A NOVENA FOR MURDER

Sister Mary Helen, aged seventy-five, had resisted retirement, fearing she'd find only prayer, peace and a little pinochle. But on her arrival at Mount St Francis College for Women she was greeted by an earthquake, an hysterical secretary and a fatally bludgeoned history professor. Police inspectors Kate Murphy and Dennis Gallagher make a very human error when they arrest an innocent. Perhaps by divine inspiration, Sister Mary Helen knows a mistake has been made and turns her own talents into a hunt for the guilty. Nothing is sacred when it comes to catching a killer with a habit for murder.

SISTER CAROL ANNE O'MARIE

A NOVENA FOR MURDER

Complete and Unabridged

ULVERSCROFT
Leicester

First published in Great Britain in 2006 by
Robert Hale Limited
London

First Large Print Edition
published 2007
by arrangement with
Robert Hale Limited
London

British Library CIP Data

O'Marie, Carol Anne
   A novena for murder.—Large print ed.—
Ulverscroft large print series: mystery
1. Mary Helen, Sister (Fictitious character)—Fiction
2. Nuns—California—Fiction 3. Detective and
mystery stories 4. Large type books
I. Title
813.5′4 [F]

ISBN 978–1–84617–938–9

Published by
F. A. Thorpe (Publishing)
Anstey, Leicestershire

Set by Words & Graphics Ltd.
Anstey, Leicestershire
Printed and bound in Great Britain by
T. J. International Ltd., Padstow, Cornwall

This book is printed on acid-free paper

To all those whose love and support have made this book possible — especially my sister Kath, who can hardly believe it happened, my friend Maureen, who bore with me while it was happening, and the real Sister Mary Helen, whose inspiration caused it to happen.

First Day

They were in the far corner of the Community Room playing pinochle when it happened. Sister Mary Helen remembered that distinctly. As usual, Sister Eileen was her partner. Over the years they had played together so often it seemed like an unfair advantage. That was why she waited for Sister Cecilia. The college president would undoubtedly be as shrewd at cards as she was at managing the college. Furthermore, it would be good for Cecilia to relax.

Sister Mary Helen looked around. The spacious room had a comfortable Sunday-evening hum. The nuns sat in small groups chatting, knitting, playing Chinese checkers. A band of devoted television watchers had gathered at one end. No Cecilia. She must be out at some meeting or other.

Mary Helen felt a twinge of guilt when she snagged Sister Anne for the fourth. The young nun looked nervous, but she'd catch on quickly. Anyone who could master all those guitar chords could certainly remember a few card tricks.

Mary Helen had just taken the bid when it

1

happened. All she needed for a double pinochle was one Jack of Diamonds, and she was positive from the way Sister Eileen's bushy, gray eyebrows shot up that her old friend had it.

At first Mary Helen suspected Sister Anne of jiggling the card table. She was about to ask her to stop when a low, dull rumble filled the long room. Then a small crack raced along the ceiling and the parquet floor began to undulate. Earthquake, she thought in horror, watching the carved statue of St Joseph teeter on its pedestal. The hanging lamps swinging in unison added a tinny, clinking sound almost like breaking glass. Both door jambs swayed left, then right, then stopped. Mary Helen held her breath. Suddenly, everything was strangely still.

'St Emydius, preserve us from earthquake.' Sister Therese's high-pitched scream tore through the quiet.

Slowly, Mary Helen exhaled. As if by some silent signal, the other nuns in the room burst into chatter. Good old Emydius seems to have done his job, Mary Helen thought, glancing at the sisters' shock-white faces. We may not be very calm, but at least we are preserved!

'We'd better check the main college building. Someone may be up there,' Sister

Anne said hoarsely, rushing toward the front door of the Sisters' Residence.

'It's Sunday.' Mary Helen prided herself on logic.

'You can never tell. Somebody may be there. And what about Luis?'

Luis! Mary Helen had forgotten about the young janitor. Grabbing her jacket, she followed Anne. Sister Eileen was close behind.

Outside, the trio paused on the front stoop. The night was still and calm, almost balmy. A lone star fell. Its fiery tail streaked the blackness for an instant, then disappeared. Earthquake weather, Mary Helen was about to say, but she remembered that meteorologists claimed there was no such thing.

Anne grinned. 'It's still there,' she said, pointing up the hill.

Several hundred feet above them, crowning the top of the hill, the massive main building of Mount St Francis College for Women stood intact. Floodlights shot through the darkness, coloring the stone building almost chartreuse.

'And looking like something out of a gothic mystery novel,' Mary Helen couldn't resist saying.

The interior of the ornate building was dark except for a light on the first floor. Sister

Eileen checked her wristwatch. 'Eight-thirty, Sunday night. That is exactly where Luis should be cleaning. We'd better make sure he's all right.'

The three nuns hurried up the moon-flooded driveway. The loose gravel crunching under their feet was the only sound breaking the stillness.

On the top step, just outside the main entrance, a slight young man leaned against one of the lions flanking the doorway. He was trembling. Beads of perspiration wet his forehead.

'Luis, are you okay?' Sister Anne reached out and pried the pushbroom loose from his clenched hand.

'Yeah, Sister.' Thick eyeglasses magnified Luis's terrified eyes.

Gently Sister Anne led him to the top step. 'Sit down. You look pale.'

Pale! To Mary Helen, his thin face looked absolutely green. As a matter of fact, in this grotesque lighting, they all looked a little green.

'Are you sure you aren't hurt?' Anne asked, settling down on the stone step beside him.

Luis had just opened his mouth when a scream ricocheted through the blackened foyer. Mary Helen's stomach gave a sickening lurch. Eileen whirled toward the front door

4

just as a young woman burst through.

'Marina, dear, what is it?' Sister Eileen recognized Professor Villanueva's secretary immediately.

'Come, please! Quick!' Marina pulled at the old nun's jacket, urging her into the building. 'The professor's hurt.' As she spoke, her slim body began to shudder.

Eileen grabbed the young woman by the shoulders and eased her on to the top step next to Luis. 'Breathe deeply,' she ordered, her chubby face close to Marina's. 'Put your head between your knees. Try to relax. We'll get some help.'

Marina slumped forward and buried her face in her knees.

Shoving her bifocals up the bridge of her nose, Mary Helen assessed the situation. Anne was busy with Luis, Eileen with Marina. That leaves only you, old girl, she reasoned. 'I'll go inside and see to the progress,' she said. Squaring her shoulders, the old nun breathed deeply and plodded through the front door into the black foyer.

'We'll be there in a minute,' Eileen called after her.

Turning right, Mary Helen felt along the wall for the light switch, with no success. A light switch, like a policeman, was never around when you needed one. Her eyes slowly adjusted to the darkness.

Slots of moonlight filtered into the foyer and illuminated the curved staircase leading to the second floor. 'The moon is a ghostly galleon, tossed upon cloudy seas' came to her crazily, as she edged her way up the marble steps toward the professor's office. One of the heavy tapestries on the stairwell hung slightly askew, but everything else looked normal. Not even one Carrara bust had moved on its pedestal. Each stared blankly ahead.

Rounding the corner, Mary Helen caught a slight movement in the upper hall. A shadow, maybe. She stopped. Blinked. Peered into the blackness. Nothing. Gripping the bannister, she steadied herself. She could feel her heart pounding. 'Anyone there?' Her question reverberated through the empty building. Silence.

'Are you all right?' Sister Eileen's muffled voice floated in from the front steps.

Mary Helen took a deep breath. 'Fine,' she shouted back, hoping she meant it. It's just the wind, she assured herself, relaxing her grip. 'The wind was a torrent of darkness among the gusty trees.' Deliberately, she marched up the remaining steps to the second floor.

Across the dark hallway, a beam of light came from room 203. Funny we didn't notice it from outside, Mary Helen thought, pausing in front of the open door. Cautiously, she peeked in. The outer office was in darkness. A second door, the one to the professor's inner office, was slightly ajar. She craned her neck. The light was coming from the desk lamp. Like a beacon, it spotlighted the toes of two impeccably polished shoes. Mary Helen's mouth felt oddly dry and parched, strangling the gasp in her throat. Professor Villanueva lay sprawled beside his desk.

Mary Helen crossed the room and squatted beside his body. Thin streams of blood trickled from his ears, encircling his head with a bright red halo. Avoiding his blank, staring eyes, she grabbed his limp wrist. It was still warm. She felt for his pulse. Nothing. His well-manicured hand fell back. Lifeless. She put her fingers on either side of his long, slender neck, sticky with fresh blood. Still no pulse.

She leaned against the edge of his desk. *Don't fall apart now, old girl.* She controlled the sob aching in her throat.

Slowly, she reached for the phone and dialed O. They would need an ambulance — and the police.

What next? Be logical. A priest. He needs a priest. Numbly she dialed St Ignatius Church.

7

Sister Mary Helen forced herself to look around the office. Everything was as she remembered it. Nothing moved, nothing different, except for the bronze statue that lay on the floor near the professor's body. The professor's body! Kneeling beside the sprawled figure, she reverently intoned the ancient Latin prayer for the dead. *De profundis clamavi ad te, Domine. Domine. exaudi vocem meam*. The words rang through the empty room.

'Oh, my gosh, is he dead?' Sister Anne whispered. Mary Helen jumped. She had not heard Anne coming. No wonder. Anne was wearing her blasted Paiute moccasins.

'I think so,' Mary Helen answered in a flat tone. Behind her, she heard Anne retch, then bolt from the room.

Mary Helen struggled to her feet, and sank into the professor's high-backed leather chair. Almost every mystery novel she read mentioned 'rubbery' knees. She had wondered how they felt. Now she knew.

White-faced, Sister Anne reappeared in the doorway. 'Sorry,' she said. Her large, hazel eyes avoided the floor. The old nun just nodded. In the silence, Mary Helen could hear the younger woman swallow. 'What happened?' Anne asked, hardly managing to get her tongue around the words.

'It looks as if that statue may have fallen on him.' Mary Helen pointed to a large, bronze figurine of a medieval nobleman. It lay on the blood-drenched carpet several feet behind the professor's head.

'Where did it come from?' Anne asked, without looking down.

'Up there. I noticed it the other morning when I was here.' Mary Helen swiveled her chair toward the bookcase. A small space at the end of the third shelf was vacant. 'The quake must have knocked it off the shelf.'

'What a freak accident! Nothing else seems disturbed!'

'We'd better not touch anything until the police arrive,' Mary Helen warned her, unnecessarily. They always said that in all the mysteries she'd read.

Anne looked at her. 'That's for murder. This was just an accident. A freak accident.'

The whine of a siren filled the small office. A black-and-white patrol car rolled up in front of the college. Its rotating light threw long shadows in the semi-dark room. A police radio could be heard in the distance, and two doors slammed shut.

Heavy footsteps clambered up the marble staircase. The outer office lights flipped on. Two of the burliest policemen Mary Helen had ever seen filled the doorway.

'Evening, Sisters.' Both officers removed their hats.

Good Catholic boys, Mary Helen observed, watching Sister Eileen sandwich her way between the men. Sister Eileen was leading a small ascetic-looking Jesuit carrying the holy oils. Somberly, the priest knelt beside the professor's body and began the sacred words of anointing.

★ ★ ★

The three nuns sat quietly on a bench in Professor Villanueva's outer office. 'Just in case we have any more questions,' one of the patrolmen had said. Mary Helen could hardly believe that it was only three days ago that she had first set foot in this room.

★ ★ ★

San Francisco had been hot. It was one of those October days in the city which make the natives sweat, swear, and bless the fog they had cursed the week before. Already the radio predicted another day in the upper eighties.

Trudging up the driveway from the Sisters' Residence to the main college building, Mary Helen stopped to catch her breath. Sisters'

Residence, indeed! Nothing but academia for convent, she thought, staring back at the plain, squat structure. It looked like the college's poor relation. She didn't know if she'd ever get used to calling that unpretentious square anything but a convent. As long as she was living on the hill, however, she figured the only decent thing to do was try.

Shielding her eyes against the glaring sun, the old nun admired the imposing building ahead. Its majestic stonework shimmered against the cloudless sky. All its windows, like so many slits in a castle turret, were flung open to catch the morning coolness. Even the gargoyles seemed to be sweating.

It's going to be a scorcher, she thought, checking her watch. Nine-thirty. Plenty of time. Her appointment with Professor Villanueva wasn't until nine forty-five.

As she approached the side of the building, voices tore through the quiet. Stopping, she looked up. The sounds were coming from one of the first few tiny windows on the second floor. Although at first she could not make out what was being said, the tone was unmistakable — anger.

'Bastardo!' a furious voice shouted.

Mary Helen hurried around to the front of the building. No matter what the language,

11

there are some words you can always understand.

'Morning, Sister.' A student passed her on the front steps of the main building. Mary Helen hesitated before the ornate double doors. Above them, rococo lanterns framed gold-leaf letters proclaiming: Mount St Francis College for Women, Founded MCMXXX.

The college! The one place she had been trying to avoid for fifty years, and now here she was. Before she could reach out to grasp the fluted handle, the heavy door flew open and a tall, curly-haired, apparently angry young man, burst past her. Shirt sleeves rolled to the elbows, stained kitchen apron covering faded jeans, he hardly fit his opulent surroundings.

Adjusting her bifocals, Mary Helen watched him take the front steps two at a time, then disappear around the corner of the building. Whoever he was, he was in a hurry.

The tomblike coolness of the foyer gave her a sudden chill. Dark tapestries covered the walls and stairwells. Pale marble busts of saints and scholars stood on equally pale pedestals. Each stared at her with cold, vacant eyes. Stiffening her back, the old nun let the door swish shut behind her.

Life goes on with or without you, old girl,

she reminded herself, so you might as well go with it. Turning right, she started up the curved staircase to the second floor. She half expected to see a knight in full armor clank down the marble steps toward her.

Sister Mary Helen took another quick look at her watch. Right on time. Lightly, she tapped on the wooden door marked 203.

'Come in, it's open,' a pleasant voice called over the clicking of a typewriter. 'Just push.'

As she entered, a well-dressed young woman, her thick, black hair clipped back severely, looked up from the typewriter. Mary Helen was struck by the young woman's beauty. Not by her features so much, although they were delicate and well-proportioned, as by the eyes. The young woman's eyes were such a clear, deep blue that they looked almost turquoise against her translucent skin.

Smiling, she rose and extended her right hand. Her hand was large for a woman's, and her grip was firm. A good sign, Mary Helen noted. 'Welcome, Sister,' the young woman said, with the hint of an accent. 'You must be Sister Mary Helen.' The old nun nodded.

'I'm Marina, Marina Alves. Professor Villanueva's secretary. The professor expects you. I'll buzz him.' With one long, slim finger, the young woman pushed the button of the intercom. 'The sister is here,' she announced.

Almost immediately, Professor Phillip Villanueva opened the frosted glass door separating his office from his secretary's. Mary Helen was shocked at how perfectly he fit the stereotype of the successful college professor. Tall and slender, he came complete, even in all this heat, with a brown tweed jacket, turtleneck pullover, and a sweet-smelling pipe. Yet there was something about the professor's narrow face that Mary Helen and Shakespeare referred to as that 'lean and hungry look.'

'Welcome, Sister.' He ushered her inside. 'We are so glad to have you.' He ran his hand over his straight hair. 'Your wisdom will be a real asset to our history department.'

Mary Helen knew bunk when she heard it. Why, the man had just met her. How in the world would he know whether she was wise or not? Unless he thought it came with age. She wanted to tell him that someone had once said, 'The older I grow, the more I distrust the familiar doctrine that age brings wisdom.' Instead, she threw back a little bunk of her own. 'I'm looking forward to working in your department, Professor.'

Professor Villanueva dropped into the high-backed swivel chair behind his desk. 'Please, be seated.' His smile was broad and practiced. Mary Helen sat on the edge of a small, brown chair facing him. His eyes remained untouched. After fifty years in the classroom, she considered herself an expert on eyes.

She glanced around the office. Like everything else about the professor, it was a study in perfection. Polished oak desk, elegant, yet understated desk set, a *ficus-benjaminus* flourishing in a muted ceramic pot, an oil painting of three mallards flying into a soft sunset.

Macho, down to the last neatly housed paper clip! She looked through her bifocals at the leather-bound volumes lining the book-shelves. Only a large bronze statue precisely placed at the end of the third row broke the symmetry.

Rapidly, the professor outlined several research projects. She might be interested in pursuing one, he suggested. She wasn't, but he didn't pause long enough for her to reply. As he spoke, he nervously clinked his pencil against his front teeth and swiveled his chair toward the small window behind the desk. Obviously, the young man had other things on his mind.

So did Mary Helen. Nonetheless, she folded her hands in her lap and forced herself to look attentive. It was all she could do to fight down her schoolmarm urge to tell him to sit still and stop fidgeting.

Abruptly, the professor stood. 'You think about these ideas, Sister. Perhaps you have some of your own, as well. We'll talk more later.'

Meeting adjourned. Ushering her out of his office, the professor gave her a big smile and a handshake. But the smile still didn't reach his eyes.

The college bell gonged out the hour. Ten o'clock. Perfect timing for her coffee break, Mary Helen thought. For fifty years she had considered her morning and afternoon coffee breaks essential. She regarded those few quiet moments she took twice daily to blow and sip and think a contemplative experience. At this stage of her life, she had no intention of changing that habit.

Turning right, she moved down the long corridor leading to the back of the building and the kitchen/dining-room area where both the students and the nuns had their meals. Separate but equal dining rooms, her friend Eileen called the arrangement.

'Glad to see you're finding your way around.' Sister Anne's voice startled Mary Helen. Curious, she had not heard the young nun pad up behind her. She glanced at Anne's feet. They were shod with laced

16

moccasiny-looking affairs.

'Paiutes.' Anne wiggled her toes.

'Humph!' was the only comment Mary Helen could think of to make.

'It's ten o'clock,' said Sister Therese, who preferred her name pronounced 'trays,' rushing by. Loose tiles clinked under her busy feet. 'You know how the kitchen staff likes us to get our coffee and get out so they can get on with lunch.'

Sister Therese did not wait for a response. In addition to being slightly high-strung, Therese was slightly deaf.

Anne spoke out of the corner of her mouth, just in case. Apparently, she had learned from experience that it was difficult to predict when Sister Therese's hearing would suddenly improve. 'I know what young Leonel likes,' she said. 'He wants us to finish coffee so he can have some time alone with his girl friend before starting lunch.'

'Who's Leonel?' Mary Helen asked.

'Our assistant cook. Sweet young man. I'll introduce you.'

'Does this girl friend go to school here?' The idea of a cook-wooing coed appealed to her.

'She works here. Villanueva's secretary.'

'Marina? I just met her a few minutes ago. She's a lovely child.'

'Right. Leonel and she came from the same village, or at least the same province, in Portugal. Villanueva helped them both to emigrate. Marina has been with us a couple of years. Leonel, almost a year now.'

Sister Anne swung the kitchen door open and held it for Mary Helen. 'We've had a lot of Portuguese here,' she said. 'Those two. Marina's sister, Joanna. She's a graduate student. The college gave her a full scholarship. But most of them work around the place. And they are very good workers, too. You'll meet Tony. He's the gardener. Probably the best we've ever had. Have you noticed the grounds?'

Mary Helen hated to admit she hadn't, so she just cleared her throat. Anne didn't seem to notice.

'There's a lot of ground to keep up. We've had four or five fellows who started to work here, to give Tony a hand. Next thing, they leave for better jobs. Can't blame them. Then there's Luis. Does janitorial work. He's brand new, but, so far, very conscientious.'

Rummaging around, Sister Anne unearthed two clean coffee mugs. 'Villanueva sponsors them all,' she said, answering the next question Mary Helen was about to ask. 'I guess he must have a good heart to take such an interest in these kids.'

Mary Helen was about to comment when Anne pointed across the kitchen to a black, curly head protruding from a row of stainless steel pots. 'That's Leonel.'

Wiping his hands on his apron, Leonel came toward the two nuns. He held one hand out to Mary Helen. She was so surprised, she nearly neglected to shake it. This mild-mannered young fellow was the same young man who, not twenty minutes before, had burst from the main college building in a rage.

'Hi, Sister.' A toothy grin broke across his face. A dentist's delight, Mary Helen thought, running her tongue over her own front teeth, which overlapped slightly.

The young man's dark, round eyes smiled down at her. There was something simple and almost sweet about him that she liked immediately.

Anne poured Mary Helen coffee from the urn, brewed herself a cup of chamomile tea, and headed back to her campus ministry office.

Cradling her mug, Mary Helen settled into the nook right off the kitchen. She had just begun to blow and sip when Marina came in. Shyly, she moved toward Leonel. One peek at the couple, and Mary Helen knew Anne was correct. Definitely courting!

19

Well, more power to them, she thought.

That morning in that nook, Mary Helen often said afterward, she had her first glimmer of an idea for a research paper: The plight of today's immigrant. Why not? There were plenty of them in San Francisco, and she had two lovely 'primary sources' in Marina and Leonel. She peeked again. The kitchen was empty.

Turning, she stared out at one of the college's well-tailored gardens. At the far end, by a low hedge, she spotted Leonel. He was talking to a young man in overalls and a blue denim work shirt. In fact, Leonel, arms waving, was doing all the talking. He seemed to be angry again.

That Leonel can surely switch from a lion to a lamb in a hurry, Mary Helen thought, watching him stomp back toward the kitchen, fists still clenched. Or maybe it's this awful heat. Refilling her mug, she started back to the Sisters' Residence to finish the morning paper.

By late afternoon, the radio was predicting a record high. 'Today's temperatures in the city soared into the high eighties,' the newscaster reported, 'topping all previous . . . '

Mary Helen snapped off her transistor. No need being reminded of how hot you were.

She rummaged through her narrow closet and pulled out a short-sleeved cotton blouse. Only one sensible thing for this hot, retired nun to do, she reasoned, buttoning up her front: head for a cool, shady spot and finish her murder mystery. Snatching the latest P. D. James paperback from her nightstand, Mary Helen shoved it into her faithful paperbook cover — one with ribbon markers and all. It was the kind seen in every religious goods store. This piccc of plastic had served her well. For years it had decorously disguised her mystery novels.

Quietly, she shut the door of her small bedroom.

The tropical fragrance of jasmine wafted down the convent corridor. Mary Helen sniffed her way along until she reached Sister Anne's bedroom. The door was ajar. She caught a glimpse of Anne seated on a round, green pillow set on a square of blue rug. Eyes closed, legs pretzled, open palms resting on her knees. Thin curls of smoke rose from a brass incense pot on her desk.

'Good Lord, Anne. What on earth are you doing?'

'Meditating. This is my lotus position. Very relaxing. You should try it.' She opened one eye to catch Mary Helen's reaction.

Mary Helen studied Anne wreathed in

wisps of white smoke. The only thing that looked relaxing to her was that hard little pillow bulging below Anne's faded blue jeans.

Inwardly, she thanked God she was in history and not campus ministry. Outwardly, she said, 'No thanks, Anne. Getting down would be one thing. Getting up would be something else again. I'm going outside to read.' She patted her paperback.

'Prefer spiritual reading, huh?' Anne winked.

Mary Helen checked the young nun's face to see if she knew. She knew. 'St P. D. James,' Mary Helen said.

'The cover's a nice touch.' Anne wriggled on her pillow.

'Late afternoon . . . old gray-haired nun . . . sitting alone with book in lap. Everyone expects a prayer book. Right?' Mary Helen asked.

'Right.'

'Then, why blow the stereotype?'

Anne's low chuckle followed Mary Helen down the corridor. At the head of the stairs she met Sister Therese. Therese simply held her nose, rolled her eyes, and pointed toward Anne's bedroom.

Oh, oh — a generation gap right in the convent corridor, Mary Helen thought, heading out the front door into the sun-baked campus.

The heat formed wavy lines just above the asphalt. Squinting into the sun, groups of bare-armed, barelegged students dragged themselves up the hill. Mary Helen joined them until, about two-thirds of the way up, she noticed a narrow dirt path leading off into the wooded hillside below the campus. She'd take it.

Prickly junipers lined the path. Just a few feet from the main driveway and it was like being in the woods. Mary Helen avoided stepping on two tiny pine cones that had fallen. The faint, antiseptic odor of a eucalyptus grove mingled with the pungent, Christmasy smell of Scotch pine. Several hundred feet up the path, hidden behind a clump of trees, she discovered a clearing with a lovely, carved stone bench.

Now here's where I could use Anne's pillow, she thought. Settling herself on the bench, she drank in the view. Before her, the tall spires of St Ignatius framed a patch of sky. Brightly colored houses with clumps of lawn zig-zagged up the Buena Vista hills. The huge television tower atop added a futuristic touch to the scene.

To her left, the copper-green cupola of City Hall stole center stage. Behind it, the sun played on the waters of the Bay and bounced off the rolling Oakland hills. Beautiful — what did Herb Caen call it? — Baghdad-by-the-Bay.

As much as she had fought coming back to the college, Mary Helen had to admit the place was beautiful. She had made her novitiate here in an old building long ago demolished when the Motherhouse had been moved. In those days, she had been one of the few young women who had entered her Order with a master's degree. Rather than flaunt her higher education, she had rarely even alluded to the degree, admitting it only when someone asked her directly.

It wasn't that she was terribly humble, or even anti-intellectual. Far from it. The truth was, Mary Helen was afraid she'd be sent to the college to teach. She dreaded the idea of being perched on this 'Holy Hill,' as generations of students had dubbed it. The college had always seemed too remote, too sterile, too academic for her.

Even as a young nun, she had known she would feel most at home and do the most good in a parish where there were real people with real problems. And, to her way of thinking, she had been right. Her entire religious life had been spent in parish schools. Her list of assignments was long and impressive. Sometimes she had served as the principal; most often as an eighth-grade teacher. Yes, every one of her fifty years as a nun had been spent in a parish, and she had loved it. Right up until this week, when she had officially retired.

Somehow, Mary Helen had managed to avoid retirement or even the thought of it for the last five years. At least, she figured it was about five years. At that time she had begun to lie a little about her age. Now, quite frankly, she wasn't so sure just how old she was. In a pinch, she reminded herself, I can always subtract my birthdate from the current year. She hesitated to do it because the difference always came out an absolute seventy-five.

This fall, however, the Superior of the Order had been adamant, initiating several meetings with Mary Helen. When Mary Helen had told Eileen about the meetings, her friend had christened them 'Leisure Lectures.' Secretly, Mary Helen referred to them as 'Senility Sessions.'

'It's time you slowed down,' the Superior had said. 'Why not return to the fountain-head? Move up to the college. Relax, Rest. You've an M.A. in history you have never really used. If you must do something, do some research.'

Well, here you are, old girl — Mary Helen watched a solitary freighter pass behind a miniature Ferry Building — one of the drips returned to the fountainhead. And nothing would do, she scolded herself, but to inflict yourself on a history department chairman who probably thinks your old M.A. and all those years of eighth-grade teaching have prepared you for nothing at all. This afternoon, however, it was too hot to do anything but rest and relax. Tomorrow, weather permitting, she'd worry about Professor Villanueva and research.

Opening her P. D. James, she flipped back the marking ribbon of her prayer-book cover. This spot was so secluded, so cool and quiet. She must remember its existence. Closing her eyes, she breathed deeply. Against the silence she heard the muted city traffic, the faraway echo of a girl's shrill laugh. Gradually, she began to notice another sound — a rhythmic scraping she couldn't identify.

Eyes still closed, she cocked her head and tried to concentrate. What on earth was it? First a crunch, then a pause, then a plop. Crunch, pause, plop. Over and over. The rhythm never changed.

Digging! Her eyes opened. That's what it was! Something about only mad dogs and Englishmen being out in the noonday sun

26

leaped into her memory.

From the stone bench, Mary Helen peered down among the trees, trying to pinpoint the noise. At first she spotted nothing. No one. Then, below and to her right, she noticed several wooden flats of sparkling ice plant. Someone was rooting ice plant on the hillside. She hoped it was the kind with the featherlike, magenta bloom. That was her favorite.

Tiptoeing to the edge of the clearing, she stretched her neck to get a better look. A ray of sun flashed against the spoon of a shovel. Sure enough, she could see the blue-denim back of a man, two large mounds of dirt on either side of him. He was planting, probably to keep the shale from slipping during the rainy season. For a moment, Mary Helen closed her eyes and visualized the hill aflame with bright, magenta blossoms. No wonder Anne claimed this gardener was the best they'd ever had. How many gardeners would be thinking about the rainy season on the hottest day of the year? And how many gardeners would have solved the problem so aesthetically?

Abruptly, the young man stopped and leaned his shovel against the rough trunk of a pine. Pulling a large handkerchief from his back pocket, he turned and began to wipe sweat from his face and hands. Mary Helen recognized the profile. It was the same young fellow Leonel had been talking to this morning. So this was Tony, the gardener. Good. Another name with another face. Mary Helen was pleased with herself. She held the theory that the sooner you could attach names to faces, the sooner you felt at home. And as long as this place looked as if it were going to be home . . .

Mary Helen was just about to shout a greeting down the hill when below her and to the right she heard the crunch of dried pine needles. Someone was coming up behind Tony. He must have heard it, too. Swiftly, he shoved his handkerchief into his back pocket and grabbed for the shovel.

A young woman emerged from between two low shrubs. She faced Tony. Mary Helen could hear the murmur of their voices, but they were too far away for her to catch the conversation. There was something familiar about the woman. She was tall and slight, with a delicately carved face. She looked like Marina, Professor Villanueva's secretary. She must be the sister, Joanna. She would ask Anne about it at dinner. Then she'd have another name with a face. Good.

From below, the tone of the conversation took a higher pitch. The old nun still could not make out what was being said. She strained for a better look. For several moments, the two faced one another. Then, flinging his shovel aside, Tony grabbed the girl and planted a firm, hard kiss on her lips.

A bit too passionate for my taste, Mary Helen thought, still staring down at the young couple. Then, unexpectedly, Tony pulled away. Shielding his eyes against the glare, he scrutinized the hill. Embarrassed, Mary Helen drew back. Good night nurse, she chided herself, you are getting to be a regular Miss Marple! At least, Agatha Christie had the good manners to let Miss Marple be bird-watching. You're just plain gawking! The decent thing to do, old girl, is to let young love have a little privacy.

Back on her bench, Sister Mary Helen flipped open her book. In the distance she heard the sounds of four feet on dried pine needles. There were no more digging noises.

The flat clang of the bell from the college belfry tolled dinner. Tucking her book under her arm, Mary Helen tramped down the path and on to the driveway.

The parched campus was deserted. Long shadows played across the buildings and the formal gardens. With most of the faculty and students gone for the day, the stately college buildings crested the hill with an aura of peace. Sweet peace, she thought, and stopped for a moment to pull in a long, deep breath.

The sudden shriek of tires warned her that someone was taking the service road too fast. A dark green sports car shot from behind a shield of trees and squealed on to the driveway. Looks like the Devil himself is chasing whoever that is, Mary Helen thought as the car sped past her. Two men were in the front seat. She caught a quick glimpse of the driver. Professor Villanueva! Why was he driving so fast? And at this time of day? What business did he have on the service road?

That was the last time Sister Mary Helen ever saw Professor Phillip Villanueva alive.

★　★　★

Inspectors Murphy and Gallagher were on duty when the call came in.

'Murder at your alma mater, Kate.' Slamming down the phone, Dennis Gallagher hitched his pants over his paunch. 'Let's go!'

'You've got to be kidding.' Kate Murphy grabbed her wool jacket and followed him out of the Homicide Detail room.

'Who got killed?' she asked, watching Gallagher hook a red light in the window of the city's Plymouth.

'Some professor. Villanueva's the name.

Skull fractured with a statue. A nun reported his body right after the quake. Thought it was an accident. The guys answering the call weren't so sure. Coroner says they're right. Looks like homicide.'

Cautiously, Gallagher pulled out of the Hall of Justice parking lot and turned left toward the college.

For several blocks, the two drove in comfortable silence. The other men in the Detail had nicknamed them 'the odd couple.' Red-headed, fiery-tempered Kate Murphy was Homicide's token woman; easy-going, soft-hearted Dennis Gallagher, its senior inspector.

Actually, Gallagher had agreed to take Kate on as his partner because of her father, Mick Murphy. A prince of a man, Gallagher always called him, and when Murphy died, Gallagher considered it his duty and privilege to look out for Mick's only child.

After two years of riding together, Gallagher still felt fatherly and protective toward Kate. He had to admit, however — though never to her — that his respect and admiration for her work had grown. Kate Murphy was a sharp gal and one helluva good cop. Her private life he considered something else again. Why, poor Mick must be rolling over in his grave. He could just hear him. 'Bad enough living in sin, but living in sin with an Eye-talian!'

'This is the perfect case for you, Kate.' Gallagher cleared his throat.

'For me? Why?'

'You went to that fancy school. You'll know how to talk with these nuns.'

Kate stared in amazement. Gallagher was a devout, practicing Catholic. She'd never noticed any hesitancy in his talking with nuns.

'So will you, Denny,' she said.

'Nuns always like the girls better than the boys.'

'You can't be serious.'

'Besides, it will be good for you to get back into contact with them.' Gallagher made a left on to Turk Street. Picking his stubby cigar out of the ashtray, he stuck it into the corner of his mouth.

So that was it! Dennis Gallagher was having a sudden attack of Father Knows Best! Although they had never discussed it outright, Kate knew he disapproved of her living arrangements with Jack Bassetti. Not that Gallagher disliked Jack. He didn't. What he disliked was their living together without — what did he call it? — 'benefit of blessing.' Denny never passed up an opportunity to extol the joys of marital bliss. *Ad nauseam*, in Kate's opinion.

Tonight Gallagher was on a new tack. Turn

Kate over to the 'good sisters.' Maybe they could straighten her out. She could almost hear her father's brogue saying the same thing.

'What exactly did you mean by that last snide remark?'

'What snide remark?'

'Good for me to get back in contact with the nuns.'

'Nothing, Katie. You've just not been around the school for a while. It would be good.'

'Good for what, Denny? For making me feel guilty about living with Jack?'

'Who mentioned Jack?' Gallagher's face reddened.

'I did!'

'Don't slam the door,' Gallagher started to yell as the car came to a halt in the parking lot, but the bang reverberated through the Plymouth.

'Sorry, Denny,' Kate grinned, turning to him. 'I know you care, and I appreciate it, but I'm a big girl now.'

'Poor Mick Murphy. God rest him!' she heard Gallagher mutter as she climbed the steps into the main college building.

★ ★ ★

'For the love of heaven! Look who's here!' Sister Eileen jumped to her feet.

Mary Helen looked up. A smartly dressed young woman in her late twenties came through the office door. An older, pudgy man followed her in. Without looking left or right, he slid past into the inner room.

'Kate Murphy!' Eileen hugged the young woman affectionately. 'How nice it is to see you!'

'Sister Eileen. I'm surprised you remember me.'

'Now, who could forget you?' Eileen turned toward Mary Helen. 'Sister Mary Helen, I'd like you to meet Kate Murphy, who was one of my favorite students. Kate, my friend, Sister Mary Helen. She's newly arrived at the college.'

'How do.' The nun extended her hand.

Kate Murphy's quick smile lit up her open, freckled face. Short, auburn hair set off her eyes, the color of fine Wedgwood. Nice face, Mary Helen thought, as Kate turned to meet Sister Anne.

'You work with the police?' Mary Helen asked.

'Kate is an illustrious alumna. Her father was with the San Francisco police for years. After graduation, she followed in his footsteps.' Eileen squeezed Kate's hand. 'She's the college's one and only police inspector. And in Homicide, at that!'

'Homicide?' The color drained from Sister Anne's face. 'But we thought the death was an accident. Just a freak accident.'

The blond, freckle-faced patrolman, who had arrived on the scene earlier and who was now leaning against the door jamb, snorted. 'Not unless the statue walked at least two feet from the shelf before it hit the guy, Sister. Inspector Gallagher wants you inside,' he said to Kate.

'Did you get statements from these nuns?' she asked.

'Right away.'

'And a list of everyone else who could have been around?'

'Yep. Plus a statement from the girl who discovered the body. Except she's pretty hysterical. Lying down now in the convent. You may be able to do better with her tomorrow.'

Kate checked her watch and then looked at the nuns sitting bleary-eyed on the bench. 'It's late, and you look exhausted. You can go now. If we have more questions, we'll get back to you in the morning.'

★ ★ ★

Slowly, the three nuns walked in silence toward the Sisters' Residence. The city lights danced below them. In the bright moonlight, the tree-lined driveway shone white. They were too emotionally exhausted to talk.

Sister Therese opened the front door for them. 'What happened?'

'Professor Villanueva. He's dead. Skull fractured with a statue,' Sister Anne said.

Therese gasped, blessed herself, and double-locked the front door.

Might as well give her the full shot, Mary Helen thought. 'The police think it was murder.' That would put quite a kink in Sister Cecilia's smooth-running operation.

'Murder!' Therese's brown eyes opened wide. 'Murder! I'd better tell the others.'

'Murder!' She pattered down the corridor muttering to herself. Before rounding the corner into the Community Room, she turned back to them. 'This very night I'm starting a novena to . . . to . . . ' She hesitated, obviously fumbling for the proper saint. 'To St Dismas! And you mark my words, before the nine days are over we'll have the' — the words stuck in her throat — 'the murderer!'

'Who did she say she was starting a novena to?' Anne frowned at Mary Helen.

Another generation gap. 'St Dismas. You

36

remember, the Good Thief. He's the patron saint of thieves and murderers.'

Anne's mouth sagged open.

'Never underestimate her clout.' Mary Helen put her arm around the young nun's thin waist. 'Look at it this way, Annie. Put yourself in Dismas's place. What would you do if, out of the blue, right in the middle of enjoying a peaceful eternity, Sister Therese got on your case?'

Second Day

Early next morning, the college swarmed with official-looking men in conservative business suits asking questions, dusting for fingerprints, making phone calls, taking notes, and all talking, it seemed to Sister Mary Helen, out of the sides of their mouths.

She bumped into them in the kitchen, in the convent, on the campus. A clean-shaven fellow with a full head of curly hair questioned her again about how she happened to come upon the professor's body. He was one step up on the hierarchy from the patrolman, she guessed. Carefully, she told him everything she had told the patrolmen the night before. Therefore, she was surprised when at about ten o'clock she was summoned again to room 203 in the main college building.

Oh, oh, Mary Helen thought, spotting Sister Therese coming from the other end of the hall. She watched, fascinated, as Therese, like the proverbial bird with rumpled tail feathers, picked and pecked her way through the bevy of police officers.

'I'm on my way to chapel for my novena

prayers,' she muttered to Sister Mary Helen as they passed each other. 'And this!' Therese made a large dramatic gesture toward room 203. 'The poor girls! Exposed to this! What must they think?' Not waiting for an answer, she continued her short staccato steps down the hall.

'They probably think it is the most exciting thing that's happened around here in years,' Mary Helen mumbled, making sure Therese was safely out of earshot.

'Come in, Sister,' a heavy-set fellow called from the professor's inner office. Mary Helen recognized him as the same man who had slid in behind Kate Murphy last night. He must be the top of the line, she thought.

'I'm Inspector Gallagher.' He motioned to the chair facing the desk. The Inspector balanced his ample bottom on the desk's highly polished top. His gray tweed suit, which had a slept-in look, strained when he reached for his note pad.

Mary Helen wriggled into the chair. She pushed her bifocals up the bridge of her nose and covertly studied the man.

She'd try not to let him catch her staring. He looked like something right out of a 'whodunit.' Already his tie was loose. It jig-jagged down the front of his white shirt, exposing tiny buttons straining over a paunch which hung slightly below his belt. Mary Helen could barely see the double Gs on the belt buckle. Gucci! She was surprised, not to mention what Gucci might have been to see his gold Gs holding up pants she felt sure must have a shiny seat. The belt was probably a gift from a long-suffering wife, or a daughter who hoped to spruce up Pop!

Perched on the desk, facing the elderly nun, Gallagher was doing some covert studying of his own. He ran his hand across his bald crown. She was certainly not what he had expected. No siree! This one wasn't like the good sisters who'd taught him at old Saint Anne's. They had been veiled, and black from head to toe, with a white linen coif hiding everything but a smooth, ageless face. Here, this old gal sat in a smart, navy blue suit, her gray hair styled in an attractive feather cut. If you looked carefully, you could still see the faint skin discoloration where her coif had once covered the sides of her face.

One thing she still had for sure, Gallagher noted, was nun's eyes. Those peaceful, piercing eyes he remembered from grammar school, eyes that seemed to be able to read minds. They came in all colors — blue, brown. This gal's came in a speckled hazel. Gallagher cleared his throat.

'Tell me, Sister . . . ah . . . '

'Mary Helen.'

'Yes, Mary Helen. Tell me exactly what happened last night. How you found the professor, who was around, everything you can remember.'

'Inspector, I have already told everything I know to two police officers. Both have taken copious notes. Perhaps you could simply read their notes. Those must be they, right in your hands.' She folded her hands and waited for his explanation.

'This is routine, Sister. Just routine.' He yanked at his tie. 'Please, if you will, start from the beginning.' Gallagher shifted his eyes to avoid hers.

'Inspector, is this a test? Are you trying to see if I am a bumbling old lady or just an old lady who still, however, has all her wits about her?'

'Of course not,' Gallagher said. Damn! They *can* read minds. He suddenly felt thirteen years old. Where the hell was Murphy? He checked his watch. She should be back any minute. Let Murphy handle it, he thought. What I don't need is another strong-minded woman on my back. This old gal might do the kid some good, too. Gallagher looked down at the penetrating, speckled eyes. And even if she doesn't, he thought, these two gals deserve each other!

'Just routine, Sister,' he repeated.

Pedantically, Mary Helen began to recount the earthquake, her running from the convent to the college, finding Luis, hearing Marina scream, feeling a presence in the hall, finding the professor's body, calling the police and the priest.

One helluva sharp old lady, Gallagher thought, listening to her reconstruct the events of the previous night. His face reddened. After eight years in the parochial school, he knew 'helluva' was not the proper adjective to describe a sister. But, still, she was one helluva spunky old gal. Must be seventy, at least. Sharp, very sharp.

'How did I do, Inspector?' Dimples played on Mary Helen's lined cheeks. 'Did I pass the senility check?'

'Fine. Thank you, Sister.' Gallagher caught the glint of humor in her eyes. Where the hell was Murphy?

'May I go now, Inspector?'

'Yes, Sister. Thank you for your help. We'll get in touch with you if we need more information. You aren't going to be transferred anywhere else for a while, are you?' Gallagher didn't think she was. She must be retired. But with this old gal, you couldn't be too sure.

'My next change, Inspector, will probably

42

be to Holy Cross Cemetery,' Mary Helen said, leaving the office.

★ ★ ★

When Mary Helen finally stepped out of the main college building, the morning fog had lifted and lay waiting in a thick roll over the Pacific. She breathed deeply, trying to relieve the tension that had stiffened her neck and shoulder blades. The campus and the city below sparkled in the crisp, autumn sun. San Francisco was enjoying a glorious Indian Summer day. It seemed so incongruous. Last night a man had been bludgeoned to death on this hill. Yet, this morning, except for the policemen and police cars and a tension in the air, the world went on with 'business as usual.'

'Hello, old dear. I was just going to look for you,' Sister Eileen called from behind her. Eileen was the only person Mary Helen knew who could make 'old dear' sound like a compliment. Perhaps it was the lilt in the brogue.

Mary Helen turned toward her friend. Dark, blue-black circles ringed Eileen's deep-set, gray eyes.

'Didn't sleep much?' Mary Helen asked.

'You don't mean to tell me you did.' Eileen

shivered. 'That poor, poor man.' Eileen controlled the tremor that had crept into her voice. 'Shall we take a quick walk before lunch? Perhaps down to Geary Street and back?' she asked. 'The exercise will probably do us both some good.'

Walking, Mary Helen knew, was one of Eileen's panaceas.

'Sure,' she said.

Silently, the two turned the corner of Turk and headed down the Parker Street hill toward Geary. Before them, Tiburon — or was it Belvedere; Mary Helen could never remember — dominated the Bay. Dozens of white sails bobbed and dipped around the massive island.

'I should have realized something had happened the moment we saw that falling star,' Eileen said as they walked.

'Falling star in the sky, sign someone will die,' Mary Helen repeated to herself. Sure enough! She marveled that Eileen remembered all those superstitions. She never was too sure, however, whether or not Eileen believed them.

'It gives me the shivers, Mary Helen. To think that someone can come right off the street into our college and kill.'

'What makes you think it was someone off the street?'

'Because the only people on campus last night were Leonel and Tony, who live here — and we weren't even positive they were here — Luis and Marina, whom we saw, and the nuns, and I don't see any of them as a murderer.'

'How do you know they were the only ones on the campus? Remember, I told you I thought I saw a shadow move in the upper hall.'

Eileen trembled. 'That's worse yet. That shadow you saw could have been the killer, and you were right there! It proves my theory, however. It was probably some crazed fellow right off the street.'

They walked a few yards in silence. 'What do you think?' Eileen asked.

Mary Helen shrugged her shoulders. No sense upsetting Eileen with what she thought. 'You're probably right,' she said. Abruptly, she changed the subject. 'Look, Eileen.' She pointed to the Golden Gate. 'Isn't it glorious on a clear day?'

Eileen smiled. 'You simply cannot be somebody's pinochle partner, old dear, without knowing when they're bluffing. I asked, what do you think?'

Mary Helen hesitated. 'I'm sure you don't want to hear this,' she said, 'but people don't just wander in from the street and up to the

45

second floor of a building to kill a perfect stranger. I think whoever killed the man is someone he knew. Someone had a reason. Possibly, someone we all know.' She stopped, astounded. She sounded, for all the world, like something right out of Nero Wolfe.

'Deep down, I'm afraid you're correct,' Sister Eileen said finally. 'But I can hardly bear the thought of someone we know being a murderer.'

'Eileen,' Mary Helen said bluntly, 'every murderer is someone somebody knows.'

★ ★ ★

The afternoon fog rolled in early. Like soft, white fingers, it grabbed Twin Peaks and quietly squeezed out the sun.

Mary Helen was restless. At the nuns' lunch table, Cecilia had presided, tight-lipped and composed. Her face was the color of her close-cropped, gray hair. Murder had been the main topic of conversation. It wasn't surprising.

'Practically under our very noses,' Therese had commented before launching into an impassioned speech on the merits of double-locking doors.

Somehow, Mary Helen felt responsible, as though she should be doing something about the professor's death. 'Nonsense, old dear,' Eileen had said when she mentioned it. 'All you did was call the police to report the poor man's death. It's up to the police to uncover the killer. Surely, they would prefer to do that without your help.'

Mary Helen knew she was right, yet she couldn't shake the feeling of responsibility. She grabbed the paperback from the nightstand. Why not spend the afternoon on that lovely little bench reading? The minute she opened the front door of the Sisters' Residence, however, she could taste the fog. Much too cold for bench-sitting, Mary Helen decided.

For a moment, she was at sixes and sevens. Then she spotted a light in the window of the library. It was perfect library weather. She'd drop in on Eileen, check out the stacks, especially the mystery section. Perhaps she'd even do a little groundwork on her research project. That would make her feel better. Almost as if she were honoring the dead.

* * *

Cautiously, almost reverently, Sister Mary Helen opened the beveled glass door of the Hanna Memorial Library. Edward Hanna had been the Archbishop of San Francisco when the college was founded. Looking around, Mary Helen felt sure nothing had been changed since.

Bulletlike lights, elaborately decorated with brass, hung from the high-arched ceiling. Dark, walnut shelves, filled with rare books, lined the walls. Brass reading lamps sat on long narrow tables. Black leather-backed chairs were fastened with brass studs. The young women studying in designer jeans and T-shirts looked like anachronisms.

At the far end of the main reading room, a large portrait of Archbishop Hanna dominated the scene. At the other end, short, round Sister Eileen worked feverishly at the circulation desk. Trying to get the murder off her mind, Mary Helen thought. She could always tell Eileen's mood from the way she worked. Why not? They had been friends for fifty years.

Could it possibly be fifty years since they'd been in the novitiate together? Eileen, fresh from Dublin; she, newly graduated from the University of Arizona. They had met at the Motherhouse and liked one another instantly. 'Water seeks its own level,' Eileen had said; her brogue had been thick, then. Maybe so, but for fifty years the two had been fast friends and, whenever possible, pinochle partners. Over the years, they had managed to meet at summer sessions, retreats, vacations.

Mary Helen watched Eileen smiling and stamping out books. Good old, plump, pleasant Eileen. Mary Helen had always thought of her that way, although Eileen was actually four or five years younger and not many pounds heavier than herself. Several times over the past few days, Mary Helen had thanked God that her friend was at the college. In Gaelic, the name Eileen meant 'light.' She certainly considered Eileen one of the brighter lights in her dim view of coming 'home' to Mount St Francis College for Women.

Waving toward the circulation desk, Mary Helen headed for the tall, walnut card catalogs. She began to thumb through the Im section. Im, Imm, Immigration.

'See Emigration and Immigration,' the card read.

Under Emigration, she found Emigration — Atlantic Migration; Emigration — Europe on the move; Emigration — Greek-American; Emigration — Life story of an immigrant.

Finally, she hit Emigration — Portuguese; Portuguese in California; and Problems of Portuguese Immigrants. The catalog card read: 'Problems of Portuguese Immigrants, Alves, Joanna.' The call number was MA 25.

A master's thesis! Mary Helen could hardly

believe anyone had already written a thesis on the subject. And Joanna Alves, one of the few names she could match with a face! What a coincidence! But then, why not? Anne had said she was a graduate student. The girl would have firsthand experience, and, after seeing her with Tony last week, Mary Helen had no doubt she had close personal contact with other immigrants. Mary Helen's face flushed at her own pun. Too bad Eileen wasn't closer so she could share it. But, then, she hadn't told Eileen about seeing Tony and Joanna, nor had she mentioned her own idea for a research project. Eileen could have saved her a lot of time by telling her the subject had already been covered. Or had it? No harm in just checking to see exactly what Joanna's conclusions were.

Slowly the old nun climbed the stairs to the stacks. Squatting down she ran her finger along the shelf. MA 22, MA 23, MA 24, MA 26. MA 25 was out.

Nobody ever reads a master's thesis, let alone takes one out, she thought. She remembered her own, which, she presumed, was still gathering dust in Tucson. MA 25 must be misfiled. She rechecked. No MA 25!

Straightening up, she headed down the stairs and over to Eileen, who was still stamping books.

'Eileen, I need some help. I can't find a master's thesis, MA 25.'

'Come on in here,' Eileen whispered, ushering her into the Head Librarian's office. Quietly, she shut the halfglass door.

'You can't find what?'

'A master's thesis. MA 25, by Joanna Alves.'

'Joanna? How strange. This is the second time her name has come up in less than an hour. Anne just dropped by. She is really upset. You remember how Marina insisted on going home last night, as unnerved as she was. Well, Anne just talked to her, and Marina is frantic. Joanna did not come home last night. She seems to have disappeared.'

'She couldn't have,' Mary Helen said. 'No one just disappears. Did Marina notify the police?'

'It's too soon for Joanna to be a missing person. Poor Marina! First finding the professor, now her sister missing.' Eileen was near tears. 'And you know, Mary Helen, ever since Anne dropped by, I've had the most dreadful feeling. No matter how I try, I can't seem to shake it.'

'A dreadful feeling? About what?'

'About Joanna. You know the old saying, 'Death always comes in threes'?'

The low moan of a foghorn echoed off the

Gate. Its wail shattered the quiet of the Hanna Memorial Library. Mary Helen felt suddenly chilled. Eileen was right. Deaths did seem to come in threes. What if her premonition was correct? Mary Helen squared her shoulders. No matter what the case, a lovely young girl was out there somewhere — maybe hurt, or maybe in danger. And something should be done about it. She'd march right up to the professor's office. The Inspector or Kate Murphy might still be around.

* * *

Mary Helen edged her way through a crush of students changing classes. Despite Cecilia's P.A. announcement to pray rather than gossip, the words 'murder' and 'professor' seemed to ring from each noisy group she passed. Trying hard to block out the conversations, she mounted the stairs to the second-floor office. Like returning to the scene of the crime, she thought. No time for melodrama, she reminded herself, nearing the top step. Joanna might be in trouble. Somebody had to do something about it.

A crack of light shone from under the door of room 203. Good! The police must still be there. Tapping lightly on the oak door, she noticed a small slip of paper attached to it. Half was pasted to the door jamb, half on the door itself — like a giant Band-Aid applied to conceal some gaping wound.

'Warning,' it read. 'This is the coroner's seal. Any person breaking or mutilating it is guilty of . . .'

She stopped. A razor-thin slit ran down the middle of the paper between the words *felony and penitentiary*. That's enough for me. Whoever is inside shouldn't be! As she turned to leave, the door opened a crack. Cautiously, Marina peeked out.

Her thick, black hair fell uncombed around her pale face. Tortoise-shell glasses accentuated the blue-black shadows under her eyes. Even those beautiful eyes seemed to have lost some of their turquoise hue, Mary Helen thought, shocked at the girl's haggard appearance. Well, no wonder! She's had quite a night.

'I just heard about your sister,' Mary Helen said. 'I'm so sorry. If there is anything I can do . . .'

Marina's large eyes filled with tears. She opened the door just wide enough for a person to squeeze through. 'Come in, Sister,' she whispered.

Reluctantly, Sister Mary Helen ducked into the room, feeling like a spy coming in from the cold — wherever that was! At your age, you should have better sense, old girl, she thought, trying hard to block the words *felony and penitentiary* from her mind.

Quietly, Marina shut the door and leaned against it.

'Are you all right, dear?' the old nun asked. 'I don't want to bother you. I just thought the police might still be . . .'

'I was just looking for my contact lens,' Marina interrupted. Her voice had a hollow ring. 'I thought maybe I dropped it here last night when I found . . . ' The rest of her sentence dwindled into an awkward silence.

Well, I'll be switched, Mary Helen thought, shaking her head. Contact lenses! No wonder her eyes were such a lovely turquoise blue. Let that be a lesson to you, old girl. Nothing is ever what it seems!

'That's a shame!' Mary Helen said aloud, glancing around the outer office. Several file drawers were pulled open. Loose papers were spread on the floor. Manila folders were scattered across the desk top. The entire office had almost a ransacked look about it. The police must have done it. If Marina were searching for anything more than a contact lens, she'd know exactly where to look. After all, she was the professor's secretary.

'It's such a small thing . . . ' Marina's voice jerked her back.

'I hope you can find it in this mess,' Mary Helen said sympathetically. 'May I help?'

Before Marina could answer, Leonel emerged from the professor's inner office. His tall, muscular body blocked the entire doorway. 'Hi, Sister,' he said, his face twitching with a nervous grin.

'Hello, Leonel.' Mary Helen tried to conceal her surprise at seeing him. 'Helping Marina?' she asked.

'Yeah, Sister. She needs a help.' Quietly, Marina crossed the room and slipped her thin hand into his.

Feeling a little like the proverbial third wheel, Mary Helen looked beyond the couple into the professor's office. A chalk outline of the man's body had been drawn on the rust-colored carpet. She saw the circle of blood, blackened and crusty now, fanning out from behind the spot where she had seen the bronze statue. She steadied herself against Marina's desk. Just like all those detective programs on television, she told herself, trying to calm her stomach. This time it was real, however.

'Sit down, Sister, you no look so good.' Dropping Marina's hand, Leonel grabbed Mary Helen under the elbows and led her to the bench.

'Poor devil.' Mary Helen shook her head.

Leonel sat down beside her. 'Poor? No. *Diabo*? Ah, yes!' Clenching his teeth, he spat out the words. His sudden vehemence startled Mary Helen. 'God let us be rid of the filthy animal.' He banged the bench. 'And do you know what else this God did? He let the animal be killed by Dom Sebastiao.' Leonel laughed. To Mary Helen, the laugh had an almost hysterical pitch.

'By whom?' she asked, hoping her voice sounded normal.

'Dom Sebastiao. The statue.' He pointed to the thick X on the floor. 'Now that is a good joke, huh? The savior of the Portuguese. Just like the professor. A savior of his people. That is what you all think, yeah? Savior? But you ask Marina.' He pointed toward the corner.

Mary Helen had almost forgotten about Marina. Turning, she faced the young woman. Marina, her face a white mask, crouched between the filing cabinet and the wall. She said nothing. Her eyes, wide with terror, pleaded with Leonel to stop. Mary Helen could almost smell her fear. Not so much of what Leonel would do, but of what he might say. What in the world was she so afraid of? What was going on?

'Jesus!' Leonel cursed softly. 'Look at what time it is. I got to go to the kitchen.' Picking up his kitchen apron, he threw the bib over

56

his head and tied the strings.

With an infectious grin, he gallantly extended his arm toward the nun. 'Sister.' He bowed deeply. 'May I show you to your coffee break?'

'But Marina's contact lens. Shouldn't I stay and help her look?'

'No, Sister,' he said, 'she will look. I will come back later to help her.'

'You're sure?'

'Sure.'

Reluctantly, Mary Helen slid her arm through his. As they moved toward the threshold of room 203, she had the unmistakable feeling that she had stumbled into the middle of something, but hadn't the foggiest idea what it could be. At a time like this, however, both she and Shakespeare had to agree that discretion was definitely the better part of valor. Silently, she let Leonel lead her from the professor's office.

As he closed the door behind them, Mary Helen caught one last glimpse of Marina. The young woman moved slowly out of the corner. Wearily, she slumped into the high-backed chair behind the paper-spattered desk. Hunching forward, she covered her drawn face with her hands. Mary Helen could not remember the last time she had seen such a look of agony on anyone's face.

Chatting amiably, as if the whole scene in the professor's office had been part of a dream, Leonel escorted the old nun down the stairs and through the dim foyer.

The two stopped momentarily at the bottom of the front steps. Several students, heads down, coats clutched tightly, hurried past into the shelter of the warm building. Leonel took a long, deep breath of fog. Tiny droplets of moisture formed on the ends of his tight curls.

'Fog, like home,' he said.

'You lived by the ocean?' Mary Helen stuffed her freezing hands into her jacket sleeves.

'Yeah, my home was near Azurara, a small fishing village in the north.' Smiling down at her, Leonel put his hand under her elbow. Gently, he steered her along the edge of the main college building on to the access road leading to the kitchen service entrance.

'Many came to this country from around my village.'

'Oh?' She studied the rugged face.

'Yeah, Sister. Many. Marina, Joanna. Tony and Luis. Carlo and his brother Jose. The two Manuels.' He counted them off on his broad blunt fingers.

'Did you know Marina at home? Or have you just become ... er' — Mary Helen stumbled for the right word — 'friendly since you arrived here?' She hoped she didn't sound too snoopy.

'It is a small village I come from. I know them all since we are children. I know Marina. She and Joanna. Not here, but in our village they are rich. I am not. They are educated. I am not. I could not marry her there. Here, I can. This is the land of — how you say? — opportunity.' Leonel beamed.

Mary Helen beamed back. She knew she was a hopeless romantic, but she loved the Cinderella story, even backwards.

A sudden gust of wind pushed against Mary Helen and twisted her skirt. At times like this I miss my long habit, she thought, goose bumps running up her legs. She was glad when they finally reached the door of the warm kitchen. Leonel held it open for her. Inside, the kitchen crew banged heavy pots against the stainless steel tables. Sister Therese's high-pitched monologue dominated the din.

'I heard that Professor Villanueva helped them all to come to America,' Mary Helen said, hoping that Leonel would fill her in on some more of the background.

'Yeah, he help us!' Leonel's eyes narrowed, and he spat viciously into the hard ground beside the kitchen stoop. 'For a price, Sister. For a price.'

'A price? Money?'

'Money, yeah. And maybe more.'

'What do you mean 'maybe more'?'

'I'm not sure. But now four are gone.'

'Gone? I don't understand.'

'Poof!' He snapped his fingers, then turned the palm of his hand up, empty. 'Gone. Without even *Adeus*'! When I ask the professor, he says they went to L.A. to look for work. But why don't we hear from them? And now, Joanna. Poor Joanna.'

'Perhaps she's just visiting someone,' Mary Helen offered.

'We tried every place. No, she is gone, too.' He shook his head, a grim note in his voice. 'Poor, nosy Joanna.'

Mary Helen was just about to ask 'Why nosy?' when a Plymouth rounded the corner of the service road and screeched to a stop.

Headlights cut through the dense fog. The harsh squawk of the police radio drowned out the kitchen noises. Mary Helen and Leonel watched, dumbfounded, as both car doors swung open.

Inspector Gallagher grunted from behind the wheel. Kate Murphy jumped from the passenger side and walked toward them.

Protectively, Mary Helen stepped in front of Leonel. 'What is it?' she asked, hardly recognizing Kate as the same smiling young

60

woman from the night before. Everything about her now said 'business.'

'Well, Sister,' Kate began in her official police voice, 'I'm afraid we are going to have to ask Mr da Silva to come downtown with us to answer a few questions.'

Kate looked over the nun's head at Leonel. Fear had drained all the color from his face. He was as gray as the blistery fog.

'I'm afraid, sir, you'll have to come with us,' Kate repeated. With the precision of a fine acrobatic team, the two inspectors whipped into action.

Quickly, Gallagher spread-eagled Leonel against the college building, patted down his sides, and slipped on the handcuffs. With a steady rhythm, Kate read him his legal rights, then grumbled something into the car radio. Gallagher wedged Leonel into the back seat.

Sister Mary Helen stood speechless, a phenomenon that many later remarked was most unusual. Kate Murphy walked toward her. 'Are you all right, Sister?' she asked.

Mary Helen nodded. 'But why Leonel?'

'We dusted that statue for prints, Sister, and his turned up.

'Only his?'

'No, but his were the only ones that didn't belong there. We understand he threatened to kill the professor. 'Crush the life from him,' was the direct quote.'

'But Kate.' Mary Helen reached over and touched the young woman's forearm. 'Leonel may have touched that statue, but he could not have killed anyone with it. Just look at his eyes — such gentle eyes.'

Kate compressed her lips. 'Sister,' she said politely, 'right now we are not looking at eyes; we are looking at motive and opportunity.'

Sister Mary Helen chose to ignore motive. 'Did you check on where he was that night?'

'Yes,' Kate answered. 'With Marina, he says. And she says so, too. They are each other's alibi. Yet she was alone when you saw her. Claims Leonel stayed in his room while she went to the office to pick up some work. You thought someone was in the upper hall, right? Could have been he. Anyway, we're taking him downtown for a few questions.'

'Ready, Kate?' Gallagher called from the car.

'Talk to you later, Sister.' Kate slid in beside him.

Even before she turned around, Mary Helen felt the silent stares of the kitchen help crowding the doorway. Their stained aprons covered the opening like a patchwork curtain. Only the small, black figure of Sister Therese, eyes wide, mouth shut, broke the pattern.

Even poor Therese is stunned into silence,

Mary Helen thought as she turned back to watch the taillights of the Plymouth round the building.

Almost instantly, the kitchen burst into a babble, with Therese's voice rising above the pack.

Foregoing her coffee break, Mary Helen walked down the driveway toward the Sisters' Residence. Poor, poor Leonel! She knew he hadn't killed the professor. When lined up beside motive and opportunity, nice eyes and instinct were hardly a logical argument. Mary Helen realized that. Yet she knew, as surely as she knew the sun would rise in the east, that Leonel was innocent. Well, old girl, she thought, squaring her shoulders, with the police making that mistake, the burden of proving it seems to be falling directly on you!

Opening the front door of the convent, she suddenly remembered why she had gone to the professor's office. Joanna. She had forgotten to tell Kate Murphy that Joanna Alves was missing.

★ ★ ★

'Thanks, Sister.' Kate Murphy replaced the phone and walked across the Detail to the small interrogation room. She called Gallagher out. Reluctantly, he left Leonel.

'That was Sister Mary Helen,' she said, replacing her right earring.

'What did she want?'

'Seems she forgot to tell us that Joanna Alves is missing.'

'Who the hell is Joanna Alves?'

'The secretary's sister. You know . . . Marina Alves — Joanna Alves.'

'How long?'

'Only overnight, but the sister is very worried. Called relatives, friends, everyone she can think of, and Joanna's not with any of them. You don't suppose something has happened to her?'

'Naw! She probably just has a boyfriend.'

'Wouldn't her sister know?'

Gallagher yawned, then checked his watch. Most of the Detail had gone home for the night, and Kate was starting to perk. He yawned again. 'I think we've got enough to hold this guy overnight. Let's give him to the lads upstairs and get the hell out of here. We can question him again first thing in the morning, after we've all had a good night's sleep.' He emphasized the 'all.'

Kate didn't answer.

Gallagher sighed. 'What's on your mind, Katie girl?'

'I was just trying to piece the day together.'

'Yeah?'

She flipped open her note pad. 'Marina found the body. Swears she was with Leonel in his room until then. If she's telling the truth, maybe we have the wrong guy in there.' Kate was thinking aloud. 'Or, maybe *she* did it. But then, it doesn't seem logical to hit him, then run out and raise such a commotion.'

'Who says women are logical?'

'No sexist jokes.' Kate's blue eyes leveled on him.

Gallagher cocked his head toward the interrogation room.

'Far as I can see, the guy in there is our best bet so far. His prints are on the statue. His and Marina's. She's the secretary. Secretaries sometimes move things. Dust. But him? What are his prints doing on it? Which, if you remember, is why we picked him up for questioning in the first place.'

Kate chose to ignore the sarcasm in Gallagher's voice. 'He claims that Sunday night he was with Marina. And he might just be telling the truth about the prints. He could have helped Marina replace the statue. The shelf is high.'

'If not, he is a quick thinker.'

'Or maybe the two of them could have been in it together. He bashes the professor, then disappears.'

'Wouldn't it seem more chivalrous for him to stay with the body and let her slink away?' Gallagher yawned again.

'Chivalry is clearly dead, Gallagher,' Kate said. 'Besides, he would have no valid reason to be in the office.'

'True. The girl says they were together in his room up to just before she found the body. And she's sticking to the story, which is one of the reasons we don't have an open-and-shut case, Katie girl.'

Again, Kate chose to ignore the sarcasm.

She ran down her notes. 'Let's see, there was the janitor, Luis Neves — says he was sweeping at the time. Officers found a pile of dirt that looks like he is either very clever or very innocent. Tony Costa is the only other person who lives on the property, besides the nuns, and he claimed he was with about one hundred other Portuguese at a hang-out in Santa Clara. I checked it out. Bartender remembers him.'

'How come the bartender remembered one guy in a crowd that big?'

'Seems Costa is a regular. Plus he gets as belligerent as hell when he has had more than his share. So the bartender keeps an eye on him.'

Gallagher shrugged. 'Figures. What about the nuns?'

Kate stared at him in disbelief. 'They were all together in the Community Room. Several verified that. All, that is, except Cecilia, the President, who was at an important Board of Directors' Meeting. Mayor's sister-in-law was with her. It's this shadow on the stairs, the one the old nun thinks she saw, that interests me. Now, I'll bet that's our murderer. Maybe one of the Portuguese the professor helped, but didn't help enough. Maybe a disgruntled student he flunked.'

'Good thinking, Kate!'

'Anyway, in case our Leonel doesn't work out, I'm getting a list of failing students from the Registrar's Office. And Marina told me she'd put together a list of people Villanueva is known to have helped.'

'We can pick that up tomorrow.' Gallagher checked his watch again. The Homicide Detail was growing dim. 'Let's take the guy upstairs and get the hell outa here,' he said.

★　★　★

The two inspectors rode down in the elevator. 'Do me a favor, will you, Kate?' Gallagher asked as they walked across the Hall of Justice parking lot.

'What is it, Denny?' Kate fumbled for her car keys, unlocked the door, and slid in.

'Will you handle that old nun?'

'Why?' Kate frowned.

'Because I've had one session with her already, Kate, and frankly, you two deserve each other.' He slammed her door shut.

Waving, Gallagher walked toward his car.

Kate giggled. Poor Denny. But then, he was not the only man who had trouble dealing with strong women. There had been her father. Poor Pa. Turning on her lights and windshield wipers, Kate merged into the downtown traffic. Fog had blunted the city. In a few minutes, she'd be home. Signaling left, she turned toward 34th Avenue — and Jack. He should be home already. She could hardly wait to tell him about her day.

On the way toward the avenues she passed the college. It had been nice going up there today, she thought. Seeing Sister Eileen and all the nuns again. She felt a little nostalgic. College had been such a safe, stable time in her life. Everything had been so certain. Pa reading the paper, ruling the household. Ma cooking, cleaning, loving every minute of waiting on them.

Everything had been so secure. That is, until her senior year. Pa had sent her to this small Catholic liberal arts college, so she would be prepared to take 'a woman's proper place in the home.'

'So as you'll make some man a good wife and a good mother to his children,' he had said. Poor Pa. Kate had to laugh. He had deliberately chosen a small, safe, liberal arts college for her. Pa had counted heavily on the 'arts.' Little did he realize that his choice would turn his only daughter, the apple of his eye, into a flaming liberal.

She remembered clearly the night when all the resentment she had built up toward her 'proper place' burst into rebellion.

Pa and she had had a terrible row in the kitchen. 'A regular Donnybrook,' Ma called it later, shaking her head.

'No daughter of mine is going to join the police force,' Pa shouted, his face red with anger. 'I'd be the laughing-stock of the entire Department.'

'Oh, yes I am,' she shouted back. 'As soon as I graduate.'

'I said, you are not! I forbid it!'

Stubbornly, Kate folded her arms.

Furious, her father had stormed from the kitchen, but not before he turned and shouted, 'I wish you were ten years younger. I'd march you right upstairs and wallop a large dose of that stubbornness out of you!'

'Don't be too hard on the girl, Mick,' Ma called from the sink. 'Remember, the apple doesn't fall very far from the tree.'

'How can you stand him?' Kate asked her mother.

'Stand him? I love him.' Ma wiped her hands on her crisp apron. 'And when you love someone, you can give a little.'

'I'll never give an inch to any man,' Kate said.

'We'll see,' Ma said. 'In the meantime, Kate, do what you need to do. Pa will come round.'

'I love you, Ma.' Kate kissed her soft cheek.

'But remember, Kathleen, whatever you choose, it's almost impossible to have your cake and eat it, too.'

So much had happened since that night. Kate had joined the police force. Poor Pa had died suddenly. Heart. Not long after, Ma followed him. Now, Kate was living in the old, peaked wooden house on 34th Avenue with Jack Bassetti. Ma had been wrong. So far, Kate was having her cake and enjoying every bite of it.

'Hi, hon,' she called, turning the key in the front door. From the entryway, she could see the light in the kitchen.

Eyes closed, lips puckered, Jack stuck his face around the corner of the small entryway. 'Kiss me, Kate,' he said in his Charles Boyer accent.

Laughing, Kate pushed the front door shut

with her foot. Eyes closed, she kissed Jack loudly on his puckered lips.

Before she could open her eyes, he wrapped her in a bear hug and carried her, feet dangling, into the warm kitchen.

Rocking her back and forth, Jack kissed her neck and ears. 'I made spaghetti, salad, and pot roast, my love,' he whispered. 'There is Dago red chilling in the fridge. Let us eat dinner, then I will eat you.'

'Put me down, you beast!' Kate pushed against his chest, which was covered with flour. 'Why don't you ever wear an apron?' she complained, dusting the white film off her blue plaid jacket. 'And don't you know red wine should be room temperature?'

'Sixteen hours over a hot stove, and all I get is bitch, bitch, bitch.' Teasing, Jack dabbed his eyes with a pot holder. Turning to the stove, he stirred the rich, red meat sauce bubbling in an iron pot.

'What a day I had, pal.' Kate slipped a butcher apron over her head and stood next to Jack at the stove. She stole a quick peek into the oven. The spicy aroma of Italian pot roast filled the cozy kitchen. She slipped her arm through Jack's, and rested her head against his shoulder.

'I was on Holy Hill all day. Made me feel a little sentimental. It was such a nice, sheltered place to go to school.'

''Was' is right. That homicide is big news.' Jack took the lid off the pot of boiling pasta and tested one strand.

'Yeah, the history professor. Talked to the old nun that reported the body. Quite a character. You'd enjoy her. And you know what Gallagher asked me as we were leaving the main hall?'

'What?' Jack held up a wooden spoonful of sauce for her to sample. His dark eyes waited for her reaction.

'Delicious. He asked me if I would do him a favor and handle the nun.'

'Why?' Jack put the spoon back into the pot.

'He says we deserve each other. She is quite a formidable lady. Sharp old gal. I like her. Has one of those faces that may not have launched a thousand ships, but she certainly is captain of whatever ship she's on.

'But you know what I think his reason really is?' Kate kicked off her shoes.

'What?'

'I think he wants to sic the nun on us and our living arrangement. He doesn't approve, you know.'

'He doesn't! Hell, neither do I. Neither does my mother, speaking of formidable ladies!'

72

'Did your mother call again tonight?' Kate stiffened. She dreaded the phone calls from Mama Bassetti. Jack was always more insistent about marriage after one. 'Marry the girl, Jackie! Irish is better than nobody. Start a family before you're too old!' Jack never said so, but Kate was pretty sure that's what Mama Bassetti said. And she knew, even if his mother had never called, that he wanted a family, too. She wasn't sure just how much longer she'd be able to put him off.

Jack turned toward her. He always looked more than his six foot three when he was making a point, she thought. 'Kate, why don't you just marry me?'

Lovingly, Kate reached up and ran one hand through his curly, dark hair. She knew that would distract him. No sense having the argument again and spoiling a perfectly good dinner.

'I love you, Jack,' she whispered, running her long, slim fingers down the back of his neck. 'And some day we will get married. But I'm not ready yet.'

Softly, she planted a kiss on his cleft chin, then one on each corner of his wide mouth. 'Smile,' she coaxed.

Slowly, Jack's face softened, and he grinned. Reaching behind, he turned off the gas burners on the old Wedgwood. 'The hell with dinner, my love.' He poured them each a tall glass of red wine. 'Dinner, we will eat later. Now, I will eat you!'

Playfully, Jack carried Kate into the old-fashioned sun porch off the kitchen. Laughing, they sank into the soft, chintz-covered couch. The Dago red on the kitchen table got warm.

Third Day

Right after breakfast, Sister Mary Helen nabbed Eileen in the Sisters' Residence. 'What are you doing this morning?' she asked, trying to be offhand.

'The same thing I do every morning.' Eileen eyed her suspiciously. 'Why do you ask?'

'I was just hoping you might be able to get away for a couple of hours.'

'And what is it you have in mind?'

'I want someone to go with me to visit Leonel.'

'Oh, poor Leonel.' Eileen's wrinkled face puckered with compassion. 'He's such a lovely young fellow. I know in my heart there must be some mistake.'

'You'll come, then?' Mary Helen asked, as if she didn't already know.

'Of course I'll come. Just give me a moment to notify my office. Someone can fill in for me. The worst thing that can happen, God knows, is that a few books won't get straightened.'

She's almost too easy, Mary Helen thought affectionately, watching Eileen, round and blue, bustle toward the nearest intercom phone.

'Meet you by the garage,' she called after her friend.

Lifting the keys off the hook by the garage door, Mary Helen automatically began to sign out on the car calendar that hung beside the hook. 'S.E. and S.M.H.' She wrote their initials in the tiny square. 'Eight a.m. until noon, Hall of Jus . . . ' She stopped abruptly. Sister Therese was an avid car-calendar reader. No sense spending an entire lunch answering questions about Leonel. Erasing 'Hall of Jus . . . ' she boldly printed 'OUT.'

Smart move, she congratulated herself, hearing Therese's nervous footsteps clipping along the parquet corridor toward her.

'I'm on my way to the chapel,' Therese whispered. 'Third day of my novena.' She raised three arthritic fingers.

Mary Helen winked. With two of her own fingers, she shot the fleeting Therese a V for victory.

'Here I come,' she heard Eileen call cheerfully down the hallway.

'I'll warm up the brown car,' Mary Helen called back.

With Eileen firmly planted in the passenger's seat, Mary Helen pulled out of the garage. The headlights cut a comet of light through the low, dripping fog as she nosed the car down the curved driveway. The fog made small, bright halos around the head-lights coming up the hill toward them.

'I can't see the cars coming in until they're nearly on top of me,' Mary Helen said, shifting into low.

'You keep an eye on the cars. I'll keep an eye on the hill.' Eileen moved forward in her seat and crossed her fingers. 'Don't worry, old dear, I'll let you know if the road disappears.'

'Eileen, if the road disappears, we'll both know it!' Mary Helen hit the bright beams.

Eileen gasped. 'Glory be to God, look!' She pointed over the side of the hill. 'I swear by all that is good and holy, someone is crouching in the bushes.'

Stopping the car, Mary Helen checked in the rear view mirror. 'Eileen, how could you possibly see someone in the bushes over the side of the hill? We can hardly even see the road.'

Carefully, she backed up and pulled over to the side.

'When you put on that high beam, I know I saw a head in that clump of pampas grass.'

Both nuns climbed out of the brown car. 'I know I saw a head,' Eileen repeated, scrutinizing the mound of bluish-green grass.

Its long, silvery-white plumes fluttered as cars passed on the opposite side of the road.

'I don't see a blasted thing,' Mary Helen said. And it's just as well, she thought, because I don't know what I'd do if I did.

Eileen shrugged. 'Well, I surely don't see anyone now.' She stomped her feet to keep warm. 'Maybe I'm just imagining things because of all that's gone on. Besides, what in the world would we do if we actually saw someone?'

'I guess we'd be accused of more pluck than prudence.'

'How does the old saying go — Pluck makes luck'?'

Mary Helen pointed to one silky plume growing just above the grade. 'It was probably the headlights hitting that.'

'You could be right. Come on in, old dear, before you freeze,' Eileen said, rubbing her hands together and climbing into the passenger seat.

After a final look, Sister Mary Helen slipped behind the steering wheel. She carefully rechecked the rear view mirror, then inched along down the driveway.

The two nuns were silent as they approached the downtown area. From the James Lick Freeway, they could see the dense morning fog beginning to lift. Ahead of them, the large antenna dominating the roof of the Hall of Justice had begun to penetrate the fog.

'Now, look at that.' Eileen pointed to the lone beam of sunlight reflecting off the antenna's metal disc. 'That has to be a good omen.'

'I surely hope you're right.' Mary Helen was thinking about Leonel. Jailed in a strange country, with a strange language — how frightened and despondent the young man must feel.

After parking their car behind the large, gray building, the pair hurried along the walkway. Passing the Coroner's Office, Mary Helen felt queasy. The coroner! The words 'felony' and 'penitentiary' jumped into her mind. She wondered when or if the man would notice the slit in his seal on the professor's door. Through the glass she noticed a hurriedly dressed family huddled on the wooden bench. One older woman, her hair still in curlers, cried softly into a wad of Kleenex. Beside her, Mary Helen could feel Eileen begin to pucker.

'Those poor, dear people,' she muttered. 'I wonder if there is something we can do to help?'

'Probably not,' Mary Helen said. 'Let's get upstairs and see if we can help poor, dear Leonel.'

A lanky patrolman in a dark-blue serge uniform held the lobby door open for them.

'Coming in, Sisters?' he asked.

'How ever does he know we're nuns?' Eileen whispered.

'Maybe it has something to do with no makeup, no jewelry, conservative blue suits, and the cross we each have in our lapels.'

Inside, the lobby of the Hall of Justice was a thick stew of people: detectives, patrolmen, visitors, vendors criss-crossed the marble floor. A baby's shrill cry pierced the din.

Along the far wall, a lonely line of men and women queued behind a cagelike window. 'Over there,' Eileen said. Above the small window a sign read JAIL VISITING HOURS, 11 to 2.

'What in heaven's name do you think we do?'

'Beats me.' Mary Helen checked her wristwatch. 'We have plenty of time and absolutely no 'know-how.' She shrugged. 'Maybe we should drop in on Inspectors Gallagher and Murphy. They'll help us out. All we have to do is play a little dumb.'

'And we won't be fooling, old dear,' Eileen mumbled, following her friend to the large, black wall directory by the elevators.

'Going up?' A clean-cut young man held the elevator door open for them. Once inside,

Mary Helen felt dwarfed. She had never realized how tall policemen were. Poor Eileen! Her nose must be a foot below everyone else's. Eileen, wedged in the corner behind several erect backs, was rolling her eyes toward a peculiar bulge on the side of the conservative gray tweed suit in front of her.

'Gun,' she mouthed.

Mary Helen nodded.

The elevator came to a smooth stop. The two nuns zigzagged their way out. Turning right, they followed the fourth-floor corridor to room 450.

From the doorway, Mary Helen scanned the cluttered room. It looked nothing like what she had imagined. Brightly colored phones, gray filing cabinets, and computer screens were scattered throughout. Fourteen wooden desks were pushed front to front into seven crowded groups. At each, two neatly groomed detectives faced one another. In dress shirts and ties, with jackets slung over the backs of chairs, they looked, Mary Helen thought, like insurance agents or realtors. That is, except for the shoulder holster and gun each man wore.

At the far end she spotted one desk with the flag of Ireland stuck in an empty Guinness bottle. On the facing desk was a lovely ceramic dish-garden full of healthy plants: piggy-back, philodendron, a touch of creeping charlie. Mary Helen knew, before she looked at the chairs, that the desk combination must belong to Inspectors Gallagher and Murphy.

★ ★ ★

Across the room, the inspectors were doing some spotting of their own.

'Oh, oh. Don't look now!' Gallagher ran his hand over his bald crown.

'What's up, Denny?' Kate looked across at her partner. He was cocking his head toward the doorway. When he did that, it always reminded her of a sparrow in search for worms.

'Who is it?' she whispered. She knew Denny well enough not to turn around.

Without answering, Gallagher sprang to his feet. She watched, fascinated, as he tucked in his shirt, hiked up his pants, straightened his loosened tie, and dropped his cigar stub into the already-filled ashtray. His mouth looked naked without the cigar.

It's either the Mayor or the nuns, Kate thought, swiveling her chair toward the doorway.

'I'll go get them, but then you handle it,'

Gallagher muttered. Crossing the Homicide Detail room, he ushered in the two nuns.

A strange silence followed the trio across the room. Gallagher introduced them to the others in the room as he went. Detectives half-rose, stiffly shook hands, and nodded. 'How do, Sister.'

These fellows can get used to crooks and criminals, Mary Helen observed, as she and Eileen smiled and shook hands. But they never seem to get used to nuns.

'Coffee?' Kate asked. Gallagher had seated the sisters on two stiff-backed chairs he pulled close to his desk.

'Please. Black.' Mary Helen answered for both of them. She was delighted that even in the midst of crisis the Homicide Detail revered a coffee break. It gave her a sense of confidence in the system.

'Well, what can we do for you today?' Kate set two Styrofoam cups on the desk.

'Sister Eileen and I would like to visit Leonel.'

'You're a bit early,' Kate said.

Mary Helen cleared her throat and stole a glance at Eileen. This was the time Eileen should have jumped in with a bit of her blarney and saved the day. One glance at her friend told Mary Helen that Eileen's mind was definitely not on the conversation.

Eileen was minutely studying Kate's beige, tailored suit. Mary Helen realized Eileen was looking for the gun bulge.

Adjusting her glasses with one hand, Mary Helen tapped Eileen's knee with the other. 'I guess we are early . . . ' She let the sentence dangle.

'But how could we ever be too early to give that poor, dear lad a little support?' Good old Eileen was coming through!

Mary Helen could feel Kate's blue eyes studying them, deciding what to do. She picked an imaginary speck of dust from her navy skirt.

'Just imagine yourself, Kate, an exile in a strange country,' Eileen began with a lilt. This time Mary Helen crossed her fingers. 'Imagine yourself jailed, bewildered . . . ' Eileen did not have to go any further.

'I'll call upstairs and see if Bucky O'Donnell can arrange something.' Removing one gold earring, Kate picked up the phone and dialed.

'Bucky's a graduate of St Ignatius,' Gallagher explained, as if the man's alma mater justified his bending the rules. 'And I don't know why she wears those things.' He pointed to Kates' gold loop on the desk. 'She must take that one off twenty times a day.'

Kate, her back turned toward the nuns, was

talking quietly into the mouth of the phone. Gallagher covered any conversation they may have heard with more loud, harmless chatter.

Sister Mary Helen could not distinguish the words, but Kate's tone was unmistakable. Kate was conning Bucky O'Donnell. She hung up, then dialed a second time.

'Everything's fixed!' Kate turned toward the nuns with a look of triumph. 'I've asked Jack Bassetti from Vice to take you up.' She replaced her earring.

Gallagher's face clearly registered a non-plus. 'Bassetti?'

'Yes,' Kate answered.

Without a word, Gallagher picked up his cigar and rolled it into the corner of his mouth.

I wonder what that was all about, Mary Helen thought. 'Before we go,' she said, 'there is something else I thought you should both know.' She paused. 'I know why Leonel can't be guilty.'

'His eyes?' Kate asked, a note of impatience creeping into her voice. Gallagher sank back into his swivel chair and laid down his pencil.

'No,' Mary Helen answered primly. 'The motive.'

'Motive?' Gallagher perked up. 'You know the motive?'

'Not exactly, but I am an avid mystery fan

and I read recently, in one of my books, that there are only four basic reasons why anyone murders. Interestingly enough, they all begin with the letter 'L.' Holding up her hand, she counted off on her fingers, 'Lust, love, lucre, and . . . ' She stopped. 'I can't remember the fourth, but I know Leonel has none of these reasons.'

Kate and Gallagher stared open-mouthed. Even Eileen frowned.

Before anyone could speak, Jack Bassetti arrived. He flashed Kate a love look that Mary Helen did not miss. Kate flashed one right back.

'Sisters,' he said, 'it's my pleasure.' He motioned for them to lead the way.

Nice face, wide, generous mouth, Mary Helen thought, stepping in front of him. Altogether a handsome hunk. Kate and Bassetti? There certainly was some chemistry between them. The idea pleased her. She turned sideways to avoid hitting the desks on her way out of Homicide Detail.

Eileen followed closely behind. 'I'll bet the fourth 'L' is lunacy,' she whispered, 'and, I swear by all that is holy, old dear, you are getting a touch of it.' Turning, Eileen smiled sweetly at a sinewy, young detective who stepped back to let her pass.

Gallagher watched the trio maneuver their

way out of room 450.

'Why Bassetti?' he asked.

'Wanted him to get a look at her. I can hardly wait to see what he thinks.'

'What I'd be interested in is what *she* thinks.' Gallagher stared absently out at the James Lick Freeway.

'Fill out, partner.' Kate pushed a pile of forms toward his desk.

'What do you figure the fourth 'L' is?'

'I know, and I'm pretty sure she does, too.'

'What is it?'

'Loathing.'

'Loathing! How the hell do you know that?' Gallagher loosened his tie.

Looking up, Kate smiled wickedly. 'Because I read the same mystery books she does.'

★ ★ ★

Jack Bassetti punched the elevator button. The three watched the red light crawl toward the fourth floor.

'So, Sisters,' he said, putting his hands in his pockets and nervously jingling some change. 'So, you're from Kate's alma mater?'

Smiling, he waited for one of the nuns to pick up the conversation.

'Yes, we surely are.' Sister Eileen jumped right in, raving about Kate and how proud the college was of her. Mary Helen was relieved. This would be the perfect opportunity for her to just smile pleasantly and take a long, hard look at Jack Bassetti. So far she liked what she saw. Bassetti was a very personable young man who laughed and smiled easily. He was impeccably dressed, she noted. The creases in his gray flannels were razor sharp. The navy jacket fit perfectly, with just enough tailoring to emphasize his broad shoulders and narrow hips.

Trying not to stare, Mary Helen felt sure his tie, which picked up both the gray and blue, must have designer's initials on it somewhere. Probably doesn't have that thick head of hair merely cut, she thought, I'll bet he has it styled! Yes, Kate and he would make a very good-looking couple. The young man was full of Italian charm, yet she sensed a little uneasiness in him. Maybe he wasn't used to nuns, or maybe there was something else. Maybe a little hanky-panky between him and Kate? Unexpectedly, her eyes met his. She could feel her face flush.

Well, actually, she reminded herself, looking away, if that's what it is, it is really none of your concern. Right now, you have your hands full with murder.

The door of the elevator opened noiselessly. Bassetti held it while the two nuns

88

edged into the crowd. His back to them, he pushed the button for the sixth floor.

O'Donnell met them outside the elevator. Bassetti quickly turned over his charges. Mary Helen thought she caught a look of relief on his face as he pushed the elevator's down button.

★ ★ ★

Hot damn! Bassetti thought, stepping into the elevator. The inspector has definitely been inspected! He hoped Kate and Gallagher would still be in Homicide when he got there. He relished telling Kate she'd been outfoxed. Kate had wanted him to look the nun over, size her up. On the contrary, he had been the one looked over and very definitely sized up. Those old hazel eyes hadn't missed a trick.

Bassetti knew Gallagher would enjoy the irony. The big Irishman would loosen his tie, throw back his bald head, and let his horse laugh rock the Detail. He liked Gallagher. He sensed the older man's disapproval of his and Kate's living together. Although they had never talked about it, Bassetti knew Gallagher wanted them to marry. Hell, so did he! What could he do? The days of hitting a woman over her red head and dragging her into your cave were definitely over.

Perhaps it was time for a new tack. Something about the little nun with the touch of brogue thinking Kate was such a lovely young woman, a credit to the college. Maybe he'd mention Sister Mary Helen picking up on their attraction for one another. He was sure he was right about that. There must be some good, old-fashioned Catholic guilt in Kate somewhere. He'd hit upon it.

Unfortunately, when Bassetti arrived back at Homicide, both Gallagher and Murphy were out.

★ ★ ★

Stiff-backed and precise, O'Donnell led the two nuns into a narrow, battleship-gray visiting room. Its only decoration was a No Smoking sign in both English and Spanish. A long counter and a glass wall reinforced with chicken wire divided the room in two, making it look even narrower.

'Sit here, Sisters.' Unsmiling, O'Donnell pulled out two worn chairs near a set of phones. There was a phone on either side of the glass wall. 'I'll get da Silva,' he said. The heavy keys hanging from his wide leather belt jangled as he walked.

'If this doesn't look like something straight out of a Humphrey Bogart movie,' Eileen said, fidgeting uneasily, 'I don't know what does.'

Before Mary Helen could answer, 'You said it, sweetheart,' the heavy iron door clanged open. Reluctantly, Leonel entered the visiting room and sank into the hard chair opposite the nuns. His appearance shocked Mary Helen. The tall, muscular body looked almost caved in. The shadow of unshaven whiskers emphasized the blue-black circles puffed under his eyes. His clothes were wrinkled. Even that curly head of hair was matted.

Leonel looked as if he hadn't slept all night. Mary Helen searched his drawn face for a hint of his usual sunny disposition. At this point, she would even have settled for finding a touch of anger. What she couldn't stand was the look she saw — one of a man who had all but given up hope.

Sullenly, Leonel picked up the phone.

'Hello, Leonel.' Mary Helen pressed the cold receiver to her ear. 'How are you?' she asked, trying to make her voice sound cheerful.

'Fine, Sister,' Leonel answered, without raising his eyes.

'Can we do anything for you?' No response. 'Is there anything you need or want?' Still, no response, although this time Leonel raised his eyes briefly. Mary Helen caught the hint of tears in his large, dark eyes. Her hand touched the cold glass wall. She wanted so badly to hug him.

'How is my Marina?' he asked, after a long pause.

'She's fine. Upset, of course.' Although Mary Helen had not spoken to Marina herself, she had seen the young woman walking around the campus with Sister Anne just before supper last evening.

Anne hadn't taken the time to change her jeans, but had just thrown her corduroy car coat over them. Her hands had been thrust deep into her pockets. Even from a distance, Mary Helen could see a grim expression shrouding the young nun's usually peaceful face.

Marina had hovered close to her, a fur-collared coat enveloping her thin, straight body. The turned-up collar hid her face. Everything about the pair said 'upset.' 'Upset' was probably a classic understatement of what Marina was feeling. Poor kid! Who wouldn't be upset? First finding the professor's body, then learning her sister was missing, and now her boyfriend being held for questioning.

'She's upset,' Mary Helen repeated. Leonel raised his brown eyes and studied her face. 'But she knows you're innocent.' That should make him feel better.

'Did she say I am-a innocent?' Leonel's dark eyes snapped. Mary Helen caught what she thought might be a hint of fear. That was strange. Obviously, he had misunderstood her.

'I didn't really talk to Marina.' Mary Helen spoke slowly and distinctly.

'You needn't shout.' Eileen touched Mary Helen's forearm. 'He may not understand English very well, but he's not deaf.'

Modulating her voice, Mary Helen continued, 'But I'm sure she knows you didn't kill the professor.'

'Why do you say that, Sister?' He seemed to be afraid. What on earth was wrong with him?

'Because she knows you, and she loves you. Anyone who knows and loves you would realize that you are too fine a young man to kill.' Slowly, color began to rise in Leonel's cheeks. His face contorted. Was it hatred she saw? How could it be? What had she said wrong? Hadn't she just assured him his girl friend thought he was innocent?

'Sister.' His voice was as cold and cutting as fine steel. 'Any young man would consider it an honor to have killed that bloodsucker! It would have been an honor to have killed the animal with Dom Sebastiao's image.'

Leonel stared at Mary Helen. She stared back, not knowing what to say. The phone

93

connection made a monotonous hum. Beside her she could hear Eileen suck in air, then wriggle uncomfortably.

With a sudden bang, the iron door behind Leonel clanged open. O'Donnell reappeared. Strangely, Mary Helen felt rescued. He laid his hands on Leonel's square shoulders. The young man slumped forward as though the air had been punched out of him.

Carefully, Mary Helen replaced the phone receiver in its cradle. Well, you were hoping he'd show a bit of fight, she reminded herself. She and Eileen stood. With forced smiles, they waved as O'Donnell led Leonel away.

Marina and Leonel baffled Mary Helen. What was it she sensed in the couple? Fear? Rage? A certain shrewdness? She couldn't quite put her finger on it. But it seemed that whenever she ran into them, she had that same uncanny feeling of having stumbled over something without having the slightest idea what it was.

Then there were Leonel's sudden changes of mood. His emotions seemed almost hair-triggered.

'Eileen,' Mary Helen said when they reached the door of the elevator. 'I have a confession to make. I knew what the fourth 'L' was all along.'

Eileen shook her head. 'It wasn't lunacy as I suspected,' she said, a twinkle in her gray eyes. Mary Helen ignored the remark. 'Furthermore,' Eileen continued, 'I knew full well you were stalling.'

'You did?'

'Of course no one can keep track of every counter that's been played during a whole evening of pinochle, old dear, and forget the fourth 'L.'' She winked. 'Unless, of course, one wants to. Why did you pretend?'

'Well, Leonel seems to have hated the professor so. Yet I know in my bones he didn't kill the man. And I don't want anyone else to think he did.'

'Could I have that, one more time?'

'The fourth 'L'. It might seem as if Leonel has it.'

'For the love of all that is good and holy, Mary Helen, what is the fourth 'L'?'

Mary Helen breathed deeply. She ignored the feeling of dread that overcame her. 'It's loathing,' she said. Beside her, she felt Eileen shudder.

★   ★   ★

By the time the two nuns arrived home from the Hall of Justice, the college dining room was deserted. Checking her watch, Eileen

95

decided to grab an apple and run back to her library. 'Just in case,' she said.

Mary Helen was glad to be alone. She needed time to sit quietly, eat, and plot her afternoon, although she was tempted to ask Eileen about her being in the library 'just in case' of what? What more could possibly happen?

To avoid any talkative stragglers, Mary Helen chose a corner table with her back to the dining room and a view of the well-manicured campus. She had been so preoccupied she hadn't noticed that the dense morning fog had finally burned off. Only one long, narrow roll still clung tenaciously to the top span of the Golden Gate Bridge.

A brave autumn sun was trying hard to pierce the mackerel sky and warm the city. Its optimism raised Mary Helen's spirits. As surely as the sun did shine, she knew she'd get to the bottom of this murder business. Of course, the first thing she'd need would be a plan — a logical, well-thought-out plan. Was it Shakespeare who had said something about logic being the 'scarecrow of fools and the beacon of the wise'? Or was it Huxley? Mary Helen could never remember which one — or the exact quote, for that matter — but the point was clear. Logic was needed. And what could be more logical than a stop by Sister Anne's office to see exactly what the young nun had been talking about to Marina?

Yes, indeed, she'd pursue the logical course, but not before she threw the little bit of salt she found on the dining room table over her left shoulder. After all, what if Eileen was right?

★ ★ ★

Mary Helen smelled Anne's office before she saw it. A light wave of jasmine drew her down the narrow corridor to the closed door. She listened. No voices, just the melodious sounds of the St Louis Jesuits' tape. They were singing something about 'If God is for you, who can be against?' St Paul's letter to the Romans. And Paul was so right. Furthermore, whose side could God possibly be on but hers, especially when she was trying to help vindicate an innocent man — one who kept losing his temper and seemed in no way concerned about disproving his own guilt?

She knocked loudly on the calligraphy sign stating Campus Minister. 'Anybody home?' she called.

'Come in.' Anne's low voice rose above the

strumming of guitars. Mary Helen pushed open the door.

Startled, Anne looked up from her desk. 'Mary Helen. What brings you here?' Quickly, Anne crossed the room and gave the old nun an expansive hug.

What's the thing with all this hugging business, Mary Helen thought, hoping Anne couldn't feel the rolls around her middle. It's always the young svelte nuns who do it.

'It isn't often one of our senior sisters drops in,' Anne said, her mellow voice teasing.

Mary Helen could have bet on that. Actually, she wondered just how long she could stay in the office before the smell of jasmine permeated her clothes.

Anne let go and stepped back. 'Come in. Sit down.'

Mary Helen scanned the dim room for a straight-backed chair. Relieved, she spotted one. It stuck out among the overstuffed, madras-covered pillows strewn around the floor. Anne squatted, cross-legged, on a pillow opposite her.

'Can I get you some tea?' Anne pointed across the candle-lit office toward a hot plate in one corner. Above it, a philodendron dangled from a macramé holder.

'No thanks. I'm not going to stay long. I

just want to talk to you about Marina.'

Anne fingered the ceramic crucifix hanging on a beaded leather string around her neck. She said nothing.

'And Leonel.'

Anne still said nothing.

Mary Helen continued, 'I've just come from seeing him. Poor fellow is miserable. I'm sure he's innocent of the murder, but something is very wrong. I have the funniest feeling that whatever it is has to do with Marina.'

Anne grabbed her crossed ankles and studied her toes.

'Anything she may have told you could help him, you know.' Mary Helen put special emphasis on her remark. That was exactly how Perry Mason said it, and it always worked.

'You saw Marina and me talking?' Anne asked.

'I just happened to notice you two . . .'

'You just don't happen to miss very much.'

Mary Helen adjusted her bifocals. For several moments, she studied the bone-white ribbon of smoke serpenting from the terra-cotta turtle on Anne's desk. The gentle strumming of the St Louis Jesuits filled the embarrassing void. 'If God is for you, who can be against?' they repeated.

Feeling exonerated, Mary Helen cleared her throat. 'As I said, anything she may have told you could help Leonel.' The scene of Marina hovering in the corner of the professor's office shot through Mary Helen's mind. 'Marina seems extremely frightened of something. Have you noticed?'

Anne bit her lower lip. Probably deciding what is confidential and what is common sense, Mary Helen thought. Frankly, she was worried. Common sense wasn't as common as it used to be. Hadn't Voltaire been the first to notice that? Well, it was as true today as when he had said it, especially in Anne's age bracket.

'Have you noticed?' Mary Helen repeated the question with as much command in her voice as she could muster.

'No, I haven't,' Anne said finally. Apparently, she had decided in favor of common sense, because she went right on. 'But really, all the poor woman did during most of our conversation was cry. And I can't say I blame her,' she added. 'As you know, it is a terrible shock finding someone's body.'

Mary Helen nodded. She understood perfectly. The shock itself had been bad enough. In addition, the old nun had been cursed with a too-vivid recall button. Every time it pictured the man lying in a ring of his

100

own blood, she had to fight down a queasy feeling.

'And of course Marina's worried about Leonel,' Anne said. 'She was with him that night. That is, until she went to the office. Leonel couldn't have done it. Not enough time. Marina's afraid the police didn't believe her. And their holding him for questioning doesn't make her any more confident.' Anne uncrossed her legs and wriggled them in front of her.

Mary Helen suppressed a grin. It was just as she suspected: even young legs go to sleep in that criss-crossed position.

'Actually, if I were the police, Marina would seem like a better suspect to me,' Anne said.

'Do you think she did it?' Mary Helen asked. Now, there was a good reason for the young woman to look frightened.

'Not from what I know of her. She seems too gentle for such violence.'

Gentle, but strong, Mary Helen thought, remembering the young woman's firm handshake and steady gaze. She chose not to comment.

'Besides' — Anne repretzled her legs — 'she had no motive that I can think of. Now, Leonel — it seems he hated Villanueva. Told several people he wanted to kill him.

Marina tells me you even saw one of his outbursts.'

'Yes.' So far, Marina's conversation with Anne had been anything but helpful to poor Leonel.

'Besides that' — Anne grabbed her ankles and leaned forward. Now for the good news, Mary Helen hoped. — 'she is frantic about her sister. Joanna didn't come home Sunday night. She called from San Jose. Wouldn't tell Marina what she was doing there. Marina hasn't heard from her since. She's called every place she can think of. Joanna has completely disappeared.'

Anne paused. 'That's what we talked about. Is any of it helpful? I'd really like to help the poor woman,' she added.

'Me, too,' Mary Helen said, without much enthusiasm. For several minutes, neither spoke.

'Actually, I asked Marina to drop by this afternoon for a cup of tea,' Anne said finally. She checked her Mickey Mouse watch. 'She should be here in a few minutes. Is there anything you can think of that you'd like me to ask her?'

Mary Helen didn't have to think long. 'Joanna,' she said. 'Just before he was arrested, Leonel called her 'nosy Joanna.' Maybe you can ask her what he might have meant by that. We could get a clue of what she was nosing into. That may explain her disappearance.'

'Elementary, my dear Watson,' Anne said.

'I know we'll be able to figure this thing out, Anne,' Mary Helen said, slowly pushing herself up from the straight-backed chair.

Nimbly, Anne rose from her pillow. 'There but for the grace of God goes Sherlock Holmes.' She gave Mary Helen a generous hug. This time, the old nun hugged back.

But before she could leave the office, a gentle but persistent knock told the two nuns that Marina had arrived.

'Come in,' Anne called.

Cautiously, Marina pushed the door open. Mary Helen studied the young woman. Her eyes were red-rimmed and puffy. Either she hadn't slept very well, or she had been crying. Probably a bit of both. Her hair was pulled severely back, making her pale, delicate face look even more strained.

'Are you busy?' Marina asked in a tired voice.

'Of course not. Come in.' Anne hugged her. 'Sit down,' she said, hurrying toward the hot plate. 'Let me fix you a cup of chamomile tea. Have you heard anything from Joanna?' she called across the room.

'No.'

'Sister Mary Helen was just about to leave.' Anne settled herself on an overstuffed pillow and motioned for Mary Helen to join her. Knowing full well when she was ahead, Mary Helen declined the offer. 'Sister was telling me about seeing Leonel this morning,' Anne said.

Marina's eyes widened. She turned toward the old nun.

'She'd like to help him. And you, too,' Anne explained. 'I have the funniest feeling Sister Mary Helen is just about to launch a small investigation of her own.'

A wan smile flitted across Marina's face.

'I'm curious about something Leonel said just before he was arrested,' Mary Helen began. No sense beating around the bush. 'He called your sister 'nosy Joanna.' Do you know what he might have meant by that?'

'I know.' Marina shook her head sadly. A lone tear ran down her rigid cheeks, and she wiped it away with the back of her hand. 'When we were children, even. She would let nothing alone. Why? Why? Always, why? In school she would provoke our teachers. She had to find out reasons for everything. After the thesis, it was the same. She had interviewed many from our country to find out their problems. She heard many stories. Some good. Some bad. Something she heard bothered her. It was like — how you say in this country? A bee in her hat?'

'Bee in her bonnet.' Mary Helen could readily understand that feeling.

'Right. She would not tell me what, but something ate at her. Then she started. Why? Why? Why? Nosy! Nosy! Nosy!'

'And you have no idea what it was?'

'None, but even Kevin was fed up.'

Another country heard from! Kevin? 'Who is Kevin?' Mary Helen asked, while Anne rose and refilled Marina's tea cup.

'Kevin Doherty. A nice boy from the University of San Francisco. She met him at class. They went out sometimes. But no more.'

'Think, Marina. What could it have been that was upsetting Joanna?'

'I have thought, Sister.' Her voice rose, and a look of desperation clouded her eyes.

'Well, all we'll have to do is study the thesis,' Mary Helen said. The solution seemed so simple. 'Surely among us we'll stumble on to something.'

'The copies are all gone,' Marina answered flatly.

Mary Helen could not believe her ears. All gone? The library copy was gone, but *all* copies had disappeared? That was impossible.

'Surely her advisor must have a copy. Do

you know who that was?'

'Professor Villanueva.'

Mary Helen was undaunted. 'Then he must have a copy in his files.'

'No,' Marina answered.

That's odd, Mary Helen thought. But after all, Marina was his secretary. She must know.

For a moment, Mary Helen was stumped. But only for a moment. 'The typist! Who was the typist? She may remember what was in it.'

'I was.'

'And you still don't know what was bothering Joanna?' Mary Helen couldn't believe it.

Marina looked weary. 'Not all she heard was in her paper. But I know it was something she found when she was interviewing,' she said finally.

Mary Helen hesitated, but only for a moment. 'Then we must find out who she interviewed. By any chance, have you a list?'

Marina brightened. 'I do,' she said. 'I typed the original list, and I have the scratch copy at home.'

'Good,' Mary Helen said. 'Could I have a copy?'

'Tomorrow. The police asked for a list of those people the professor helped. When I come to do that, I'll make you a copy of the people Joanna interviewed.'

106

'That would be wonderful,' Mary Helen said.

Anne studied the toes of her Paiute moccasins. 'And could you also get us' — the words seemed to stick in the young nun's throat — 'a copy of the list you're giving to the police?' Well, I'll be switched, Mary Helen thought, biting the insides of her cheeks to keep from grinning. Even Anne was getting into the investigation business.

Wide-eyed, Marina nodded. 'If it will help,' she said.

'Well, at this point it won't hurt,' Anne said, then giggled. 'Don't tell me I've caught a touch of Mary Helen?'

Suddenly, the little color left in Marina's face drained. Her slim body swayed. Lunging forward, Anne grabbed her upper arms and bent the young woman forward, head between her knees.

'Have you eaten today?'

'No.'

'Come on, my friend,' Anne said, carefully helping Marina to her feet and putting her long arm firmly around Marina's shoulders. 'We are going posthaste to the Hungry Mouth!'

Mary Helen watched the two tall, slim young women, like a matched pair, edge down the long corridor.

After a quick trip to her small bedroom, Mary Helen set out up the driveway. She had decided to head for that secluded stone beach on the hillside and ponder the next step in her plan. 'I'll think till I'm weary of thinking,' she thought. She had brought along her faithful plastic-covered paperback to read if and when that happened. She hoped no one had beat her to 'her spot.'

My spot! She smiled. Good night, nurse! A week ago, she hadn't even known the spot existed. Now it was hers! If she wasn't careful, pretty soon she'd begin to think she belonged here!

'Whew,' Mary Helen sighed audibly when she finally reached the stately clump of trees. The air had a crisp sting, but the sun brimmed the clearing. Its rays illuminated the drooping acacia, bowed with golden clusters. She sat down hard on the cold stone bench.

Crossing her legs at the ankles, Mary Helen took one long, luxurious stretch. The sun felt warm and friendly on her back. Let your mind wander freely, she reminded herself. Eliminate the impossible; test the improbable. That's what Charlie Chan seemed to do in his cases. And somehow, his answers always popped up just in time to reveal it to Number

One Son. She'd try it.

First, what is it I really know? she asked herself. Well, she knew there was a dead body. A vivid picture of Professor Villanueva, white and limp, a thin stream of blood trickling from each ear, shot through her mind. She felt the usual wave of nausea. Enough of that!

She struggled to rid her mind of that awful image. What do I need to know? she asked herself. What I need to know is who had the opportunity and the motive.

Opportunity? Obviously, Luis the janitor and Marina both had that. Poor Luis. She remembered how ghostly pale and shaken he had been. Was it the earthquake that had frightened him, or had he seen something else? And what about Marina? The young woman had been near hysteria. But, who wouldn't be — finding a dead body in a halo of blood? What had Marina been doing in the office so late at night? In fact, what had she and Leonel been doing in that office yesterday? Were they really looking for a contact lens? As much as the old nun wanted to believe it, that was a bit hard to swallow. Then, what were they doing there? Mary Helen would have to find out.

Suddenly, the damp cold of the stone bench began to seep through her navy polyester skirt. She was chilled. Too bad the sun was losing its battle. A thick, gray wall of fog had begun to roll back in from the Gate. She had better get up and walk. Walking would warm her up, and maybe even help her unclutter her mind.

Leaving the small clearing, Mary Helen clutched her paperback and started down the winding dirt path through the trees. Around her, the eucalyptus made a soft swish as the wind ruffled the narrow, pointed leaves. Their gentle whisper was soothing, like a consoling presence. Which reminded her — what about that other presence, the one she had sensed in the darkened hallway? Had it just been her imagination, or had it been real? And if real, who had it been?

Then there was motive. Who had a motive? Leonel hated the professor. She had already decided that Leonel wasn't the murderer. Therefore, someone else must have a motive, too.

Someone out there. Mary Helen paused and surveyed the side of the hill. But who? Everything appeared so peaceful, so unsullied, so 'lovely, dark, and deep.' 'But I' — she gazed at Tony's freshly rooted ice plant and recited Frost aloud — 'I have promises to keep, and miles to go before I sleep.' Well, at least she had several hundred yards to go. And so many questions! She must not forget this Dom Sebastiao business, whoever he was. One thing she did know for an absolute fact was that the professor had not killed himself!

From the Bay, a foghorn sounded a mournful groan. Without warning, a cloud covered the sun. Mary Helen shivered. She folded her arms even more tightly, trying to fight off the damp chill.

Behind her on the path, she heard the twigs crackling. Someone was walking. She turned, ready to greet whomever it was. No one. Silence. She walked a few yards more, and listened. Below her, off the path, she heard the rustle of dried pine needles. Maybe a small animal was scurrying for shelter. She searched the wooded hillside. A long shadow fell from behind a tree. Was it the form of a man, or just a low-slung branch from a pine? Mary Helen adjusted her glasses for a better look. Nothing. Must be just a sudden gust of wind moving the trees.

Suddenly, coming toward her, she heard the crunching of gravel. She waited, stone still, expecting to see someone. No one. Again, silence.

'Hello,' she called loudly. Her palms felt damp with fear. No answer. Just the faint echo of her own voice mingled with the low groan of the foghorns from the Bay.

Impulsively, Mary Helen turned and ran up the dirt path. Her feet slipped on the small stones. Prickly junipers snagged her nylons. Her breath came in short, sharp gasps. When she finally reached the clearing, she sat on the stone bench.

Calm down, old girl, calm down. She tried to soothe her nerves. Breathe deeply. She rubbed her knees. Not only did she have 'rubbery knees'; right now they felt as if they were plain water. This is nonsense, she reminded herself, taking another deep breath. You have allowed this murder business to get the best of you. Now, what on earth are you afraid of? And who on earth would be out to harm you?

She decided, however, with a sudden surge of largesse, that tonight she'd throw in an extra prayer or two to St Dismas. No harm at all in giving Sister Therese a hand.

Mary Helen was relieved to hear the loud, friendly gong of the college bell calling everyone to supper. This time, she'd be happy that the dining room was not deserted.

Fourth Day

Mary Helen overslept. She never overslept. She was surprised and, frankly, annoyed. When she awoke, the alarm clock said 10:10, yet her bedroom was still dark. One peek out the narrow window told her why. A thick cushion of fog blunted the peaks of the hills. Slowly, the fog was rolling down, blotting out the entire neighborhood. Only the tip of Sutro Tower pierced the denseness.

'Drooping fog as black as . . . whatever,' the old nun grumbled, unable to recall Shakespeare's simile. But the 'drooping' and 'black' part was applicable enough. The chill in the room forced her to dress quickly. Pushing aside her polyester jackets, she pulled out the bulky, Aran knit sweater Eileen had brought her from Ireland on her last visit home. Today was definitely Aran Isles weather. The sweater would be perfect.

Slamming the heavy convent door shut behind her, she hurried across the campus toward the kitchen. The fog had changed to a light rain. Small groups of wind-blown students dashed past. Shivering, Mary Helen pulled the collar of the sweater around her ears.

'Hi! I missed you this morning. Are you feeling okay?' a cheerful voice asked. Anne! Blast! Mary Helen hadn't heard her coming up from behind.

'I'm fine. I just overslept. This fog is downright depressing.'

'Last weekend when it was so hot, we were all wishing for it.'

'That was last weekend,' Mary Helen said, pulling her wool sweater even tighter around her.

Anne laughed. 'You're beginning to sound like a real native.'

That thought was even more depressing.

'Did you have breakfast?' Mercifully, Anne changed the subject.

'I'm on my way to get a cup of coffee now.'

'I wish I could join you. I talked with Marina at dinner last night, and there are some things I want to share.'

Share? Why don't we just *tell* any more? Mary Helen wondered.

'But I have appointments all day long,' Anne said, checking her Mickey Mouse watch. 'Can you stop by my office late this afternoon?'

'Did you find out more about Joanna?' Mary Helen couldn't wait.

'Not really. That is, not what she was nosing into, but more about who she was nosing into it with!'

Untangling that sentence before her first cup of coffee was too much for Mary Helen, so she let it pass. 'Atta girl,' she said simply. Anne winked, and took the short cut through a side door of the main college building to her office.

Sweater collar up, head down, Mary Helen swung the kitchen door open. With a short, shrill gasp, Sister Therese scooted back.

'I'm so sorry,' Mary Helen apologized, relieved she hadn't struck the slight nun with the wooden door — she was counting on Therese's novena. 'How's your novena going?'

'I finished today's prayers,' Therese said, obviously thrilled that someone was interested. 'Very early this morning.'

Did she really emphasize the *very*, and *early*, Mary Helen wondered, glaring at the sparrowlike figure vanishing around the corner, or was it just my imagination? She poured herself a cup of strong black coffee.

* * *

Sister Mary Helen spent the better part of the day in the stacks of Hanna Memorial Library. Armed with a pencil and scratch pad, she commandeered a vacant carrel in the 914 section.

'What on God's green earth are you doing back here?' Eileen whispered when she finally noticed her friend. Mary Helen was surrounded by three stacks of books, two tall and one short.

'Looking up Dom Sebastiao,' she said, scanning the index of one large, dusty volume.

'Who?'

'Dom Sebastiao. Remember? The fellow Leonel mentioned, the one whose statue killed the professor? I've never heard of him, and I'm curious.'

'Are you having any luck?' Eileen asked, picking up a thin volume from the shortest pile. Flipping to the index, she ran her stubby finger down the page.

'Not too much.' Mary Helen patted the two tall stacks of books. 'I've been through both these piles,' she said. 'I've just these left.' She pointed to the shortest stack.

'Not a mention here.' Eileen added her book to the 'been-through' pile.

'Although I don't know much, I know more than I knew.' Mary Helen said.

'Now, what is it you know?' Eileen leaned against the carrel.

Mary Helen ran down the scribbled notes on her pad. 'I know Dom Sebastiao was a twenty-four-year-old king who sailed out of

Portugal in 1578 to conquer Morocco from Mulei Abde Almelique. He took twenty-three thousand men with him. Seems the old counselors thought it was a crazy idea. Almelique didn't look so kindly on it, either.'

'You can never tell these kids anything,' Eileen said.

'After one terrible battle in North Africa, it was all over. Only fifty soldiers escaped. Over eight thousand lay dead. The rest were taken captive.'

'What happened to Dom Sebastiao?'

'Last seen, he was fighting, sword in hand. His body was never recovered. For years people hoped he was alive and would return.'

'Interesting,' Eileen said.

'This is the interesting part.' Mary Helen read directly from her notes. 'Sebastianismo became a cult in Portugal, one that still lingers on. It embodies not only all the yearning summed up in the word *saudade*, but also a leaning toward insane exploits based on the fantastic hope that by some miracle they might succeed.'

Clearing her throat, she continued, 'Sebastianismo also involves a kind of messianic belief that one day there will appear a liberator from oppression.' Mary Helen put down her note pad. 'Yesterday, Leonel told us it would be an honor to kill the professor with the statue. I guess he considered the professor the oppressor.'

'It seems he did.' Eileen examined the half-empty shelf next to the carrel. 'Look at all that dust between 914.69 and 914.70!' she said. 'Amazing, isn't it? As long as you have all those books out, I think I'll run and get my dust rag.'

Mary Helen's eyebrows arched. 'I'm talking murder; you're talking dust?'

'I've murder up to here.' Eileen touched the top of her head, turned on her heel, and rushed to her desk for the rag and the Endust.

Good old Tidy-paws! Mary Helen remembered that cleaning, like walking, was one of Eileen's panaceas. These days she must have the cleanest library in Christendom.

Mary Helen went back to skimming indexes. For an hour, she pored over everything in the 914.69 section, the 946.90 history section, the reference section, and even the encyclopedia. Finally, yawning, she stretched and left the stacks. From the main door, she waved goodbye to Eileen, who was dusting something at the circulation desk.

Slowly, Sister Mary Helen moved down the dark, high-arched corridor that ran between the library and the chapel. Her mind and muscles were cramped.

What she needed was some fresh air. But first she'd make a quick visit to the chapel — give Sister Therese a hand. Then she'd get her mystery book and, cold or no cold, sit outside and read.

The old nun pulled open the bronze chapel door. Immediately, she caught the comfortable aroma of incense mingled with wax. The sudden contrast between the lighted corridor and the dim chapel blinded her. Only the lone, red flicker of the sanctuary lamp shone in the semidarkness.

Genuflecting, Mary Helen slipped into a back pew. The chapel was warm and quiet. The late afternoon sun illuminated the majestic stained glass windows lining the west wall. For several moments she sat, breathing deeply, drawing in all the peace and serenity of the gothic eminence. When her eyes had finally adjusted to the light, Mary Helen noticed she was not alone.

In one of the front pews, before the main altar, a young woman knelt. She was hunched over, her forehead resting on the bench in front, her ebony hair fanned out.

Must have come in before I did, Mary Helen thought. Squinting in the dim light, she studied the woman. Probably a student. But the figure remained so still, so rigid, Mary Helen began to worry. That is a strange position to pray in, she thought, and must be terribly uncomfortable. Kneeling, she hunched over and pressed her own forehead against the bench in front. It took only a minute of testing the position for her to be convinced something was definitely wrong.

Rising from her pew, she hurried up the center aisle. She cleared her throat several times, hoping not to startle the young woman. The figure did not move. Very gently, she touched the thin shoulder.

With a thud, the woman's head slid off the bench, and her body fell. It wedged between the bench and the padded kneeler. Both arms stuck straight up in the air. Mary Helen had read enough crime novels to know rigor mortis when she saw it. Yet the legs dangled loosely. Whoever had stuffed the stiffened body into the pew must have broken the rigor in her knees. Mary Helen retched.

Sightlessly, the young woman stared up at her. The right side of her skull had been smashed, and a sickening clot of dried blood was splashed across her delicate face. Mary Helen recognized the face — it was Joanna.

Those two thin legs hung as loosely as a rag doll. Joanna had died the death of a rag doll. Mary Helen closed her eyes, hoping to blot out the sight. Instead, an image of the professor lying in a bloody halo flashed before her.

Mary Helen didn't remember screaming. Yet she must have. Her mouth was open, her throat dry and sore. An agonizing shriek reverberated through the nave and resounded in her ears.

She lurched down the middle aisle. Her footsteps hit hard against the waxed parquet squares, their echo ringing through the empty chapel.

She leaned against the heavy, bronze door. Calm down, old girl, she cautioned herself, trying to catch her breath. Think sensibly. First things first. Phone. Yes, phone. Where was the nearest phone? It took her a moment to remember. In Eileen's library, of course.

Throwing open the chapel door, Mary Helen turned left and headed down the deserted corridor. Thank God most of the girls were gone. No sense in alarming everyone. This might be a dream. All this might be part of a long, cruel dream. By the time she reached the door of the library, she was panting.

'What happened?' Eileen asked as soon as she saw Mary Helen's face.

'Let's go into your office,' Mary Helen whispered, trying hard to keep calm. Several stragglers were studying at the long, oak table. 'I don't want to be overheard. I've found a body in our chapel.'

Eileen followed her into the small room. Closing the door, she sank into a chair. Her gray eyes were wide.

Mary Helen headed straight for the phone on the desk. Robotlike, she picked up the receiver and dialed O. 'I found a body. I think it's Joanna.' She stopped. Eileen blessed herself. 'Yes, Operator.' Mary Helen's voice was steady. 'Please may I have the police. Homicide, please. Yes, it is an emergency.'

★   ★   ★

Mary Helen hung up. Walking to the water cooler, she filled two Dixie cups. 'I wish this was something stronger,' she said, offering one to her friend. Only then did she notice that her hand was trembling.

'Come, sit down.' Eileen patted the chair across from her.

Silently, the two nuns sat facing one another. Each sipped water from her paper cup. Both strained to hear the high-pitched screech of the police siren coming up Turk Street.

★   ★   ★

'You aren't going to believe this, Denny.' Kate Murphy hung up the phone and quickly replaced her right earring.

'Try me.' Gallagher looked up from the stack of papers on his desk.

'That was Sister Mary Helen.'

'What's up with her?'

'She found another body. A young woman in the college chapel.' Kate grabbed her jacket from the back of her chair.

'What the hell is this world coming to?' Gallagher sputtered, leading the way out of the Homicide Detail. 'Is there no place sacred any more?' he asked to no one in particular. Following him, Kate smiled. Bizarre homicides always threw Gallagher into a barrage of clichés.

With sirens screaming from their vehicle, the two inspectors maneuvered their way through rush-hour traffic toward Mount St Francis College for Women. 'Wait till the papers get hold of this,' Gallagher said.

'Papers, nothing! Wait till the Chief hears. His daughter is an alumna, and the Mayor's sister-in-law is on the Board of Directors!'

★ ★ ★

For a long time, the two nuns sat in heavy silence, waiting for the police to arrive. A

123

sudden gust of wind howled against the metal weather stripping. Its mournful wail filled the small library office.

Quick tears welled up in Eileen's eyes. They ran down her pudgy cheeks. 'That's the second death,' she said.

Mary Helen fumbled for a Kleenex. 'Almost new.' She handed her friend two crumpled pieces of tissue. Eileen bent over and began to sob. Clapping her hands over her ears, Mary Helen let her weep.

Several minutes later, a car slammed to a stop in front of the building, and two doors banged shut. The hollow, metallic sound floated up to the silent office. Mary Helen peered out.

'They're here.' And, thank God, she thought, they didn't use the siren on the hill.

'Do you think we should go out to meet them?' Eileen asked.

'Better wait right here. They know where we are.'

'Have all the students left the library?' Eileen asked, dabbing her red-rimmed eyes. 'I'd hate to meet any of them.'

From the half-glass office door, Mary Helen surveyed the reading room. 'The place is' — she swallowed the urge to say *dead as a doornail* — 'deserted'.

The main door of the library swung open,

and Kate Murphy clipped across the long room toward the office. Gallagher stopped long enough to stuff his cigar stub into the metal cannister. Then he followed Kate. Mary Helen was relieved to see them both. Quickly she threw open the door. 'Here we are,' she whispered. Her voice filled the vacant room.

'Sister, are you all right?' Kate asked as soon as she was close enough to get a good look at the old nun's face. 'You look as white as a ghost.'

'Fine.' Mary Helen wished the young woman had thought of another figure of speech.

'You said the body was in the chapel?'

'That's right. In the front pew.'

Gallagher stepped back deferentially. 'Sister, will you take us there, please?'

Sister Mary Helen took the lead. Silently, the other three followed her into the hall.

Long shadows webbed the walls and floor in the narrow corridor. The click of Kate's high heels echoed through the silent building. A sudden chill ran up Mary Helen's spine. How can a place be so alive and vibrant one minute, she wondered, and so dead and desolate the next?

When the four finally reached the chapel door, Gallagher flung it open. The familiar odor of wax and incense greeted them. They

125

stepped inside. Slowly, the heavy door closed, leaving them adjusting to the semi-darkness.

Everything looked so quiet, so peaceful, so ordinary. Maybe she had just imagined everything, Mary Helen hoped. Maybe it really hadn't happened. Maybe . . . On the main altar, the sanctuary lamp sputtered and popped, throwing a finger of light on a thin, white arm. The body was there. She had not imagined it. Beside her, Eileen trembled. Her single sob filled the vast emptiness. Gallagher plunged down the middle aisle. 'Get the overhead lights,' he ordered, loosening his tie.

'They are in the sacristy,' Eileen whispered, then sank into the back pew.

'That's the room next to the altar.' Mary Helen pointed toward the small door to the right of the altar.

Pivoting, Kate hurried up a side aisle. Moments later, the electric candelabra flipped on overhead. Muted light flooded the nave.

'Sister, could you by any chance identify this young woman for us?' From the front, Gallagher's voice echoed through the chapel.

Mary Helen faced her friend. Eileen's color was gone. Yet her Irish jaw was firmly set, her gray eyes determined. 'We've no choice but to be brave,' Eileen whispered.

'Then it's brave we'll be.' Mary Helen

patted Eileen's hand. Deliberately, Eileen rose from the hard pew. Steadying herself against the bench, she linked arms with her friend. Fighting down a sudden sweep of nausea, Mary Helen forced herself to accompany Eileen up the middle aisle toward the corpse.

The two nuns skirted the bony hand grasping lifelessly at the marble. They joined Kate and Gallagher in a small, tight circle hovering over the crumpled body.

'It's Joanna. Joanna Alves,' Eileen whispered hoarsely. Moving back, she leaned against the altar rail.

I hope she didn't see those thin dangling legs, Mary Helen thought, moving back with her friend. Gently she put her arm around Eileen's shoulders.

'Are you two okay?' Gallagher asked the nuns. Without waiting for an answer, he turned toward Kate. 'I'll get the boys,' he said. 'You take care of these two.'

Lumbering toward the side exit, Gallagher shook his head. 'Jeez, is no place sacred any more?' he grumbled. Before he reached the exit, he pulled a fresh cigar from his inside pocket. He stuck it into the corner of his mouth. The exit door was only half closed when he struck a match against the outside chapel wall. Cupping his hands, he protected the flame from a quick gust of wind.

'Goddam,' he exploded. His curse rang through the chapel. 'Goddam, no place is sacred any more!'

'Come on, Sisters, let's go into the sacristy,' Kate said, rising from beside Joanna's broken body. Mary Helen noticed Kate's gaze pause sympathetically on each of their faces. 'The boys will be here in a few minutes to take care of things,' she said. 'We can talk inside. Besides, you two had better sit down for a few minutes. Murder isn't your usual line.'

I hope to heaven she's right, Mary Helen thought, letting Kate shepherd them across the sanctuary. 'We're both fine,' she reassured the young woman. She noticed, however, that when she stopped in front of the tabernacle to genuflect, her knees wobbled.

Once they were settled in the small anteroom, Kate turned toward Mary Helen.

'That's the girl you reported missing, isn't it?' Kate asked.

The old nun nodded her head. 'She didn't come home last Sunday night, and no one had heard from her since,' Mary Helen said. 'And now we know why.'

'The deceased was the sister of Marina Alves, Professor Villanueva's secretary?' Kate checked the facts with Eileen.

'Yes.' With the back of her hand, Eileen

caught a single tear escaping down her cheek. 'I'm sorry,' she said, 'but I can't seem to stop crying.'

Without comment, Kate turned her attention toward Mary Helen. 'How did you happen to find the body?' she asked.

Quickly, Mary Helen recounted her research on Dom Sebastiao and her pop-in visit to the chapel.

'Interesting!' was the only remark Kate made at the end of the entire recitation.

'I'll tell you what else is interesting,' Mary Helen said. 'That the old expression is true! You know, the one — 'It's an ill wind that blows no good.''

'What exactly do you mean, Sister?'

'At least one good thing has come from this tragedy,' Mary Helen said.

'And what exactly is that?' Eileen looked amazed.

'Leonel. I was right about Leonel. He couldn't have killed the girl. He is still in jail.'

Kate studied Sister Mary Helen. 'I hate to break this to you, Sister,' she said, leaning her head against the sacristy wall, 'but your friend, Leonel, was released from the sixth floor this morning.'

★　★　★

Out on 34th Avenue, Jack Bassetti was busy preparing a candlelight supper. He'd taken the day off so he would have plenty of time. Tonight, he intended to propose to Kate. Again! He took the leaves out of the dining room table to make a small intimate circle.

Standing back, Jack admired his handiwork. The delicate Bavarian china looked both romantic and domestic. Just the right touch. He was glad he'd remembered the Waterford crystal. The flickering candles caught the sharp cuts in the wineglasses. Kylemore, Kate had called the pattern. Named after a large abbey of nuns. Good touch. Furthermore, they had been her mother's. A little sentimentality never hurt.

No flowers, Jack decided. That decision was easy for him to make. First of all, he didn't know how to arrange flowers. Second, how could you hold hands across a table with flowers plunked right in the middle? Handholding was definitely in his plan. Flowers were out.

Mentally, Jack ran down his list: table set, wine cooling, martinis in glass pitcher in fridge, Chinese from Yet-Wah's in oven. That last item bothered him. Take-out Chinese food lacked a certain romance. But, he reasoned, the Chinese people must propose to one another over egg roll. Look how many

Chinese there were!

Atmosphere! That was the one thing missing. Jack pulled the long chain on the glass chandelier in the living room. Off! He lit the large candle on the coffee table. Perfect. Now to block out the noise of the traffic on Geary Street. He had just tuned in KFOG when he heard Kate's footsteps on the front porch.

Gently, Jack planted a light kiss on her neck.

'Are you okay?' he asked. She looked exhausted.

'Yes, I'm okay. Just beat,' she said. Her slender body sagged against him. She let him take off her jacket and put her purse and gun in the hall closet.

'You'll never believe the day I had.'

'You'll never believe the night I have planned,' Jack said, taking her in his arms. Slowly, he moved her in a smooth dance step from the entrance hall into the living room.

'Good grief, pal.' Kate gazed around the candle-lit living room. 'Did we forget to pay the P.G. and E.?'

Ignoring her remark, Jack hummed softly. Getting her to accept his proposal wasn't going to be any easier even with his added romantic ambience. Maybe he should wait till she had a better day. Hell, he thought, twirling her into a dip, when could he ever count on Homicide having a good day?

'My feet are killing me,' Kate whispered.

'Let me sweep you off your feet,' Jack whispered back.

'Let me take my shoes off.'

Good old practical Kate, Jack thought, his eyes following her up the stairs; it was part of her charm — and part of what made her so damn frustrating.

While she was getting her bedroom slippers, Jack poured the martinis.

'To us,' he said, handing her a long-stemmed glass.

'To us.' Kate sank into the overstuffed couch by the front windows. Jack sat beside her. Silently, they each took a sip. The candle threw soft shadows across Kate's freckled face. Putting her glass on the coffee table, she began to twist a strand of hair around her index finger, then push it into a tight curl. Jack recognized the infallible sign. She was thinking hard.

'A penny for your thoughts.'

'You'll want your money back.'

'Try me,' Jack said, afraid she might be right.

'I know we agreed to try not to bring work home.'

'You must admit rape and murder do not

make for relaxing dinner conversation.'

Kate smiled. 'But I just can't get today off my mind.'

Jack took another sip of his martini. His eyes paused on her face. 'Okay,' he said, 'let's have it. What happened?'

'We had another murder at the college. Hasn't it made TV yet?' Kate picked up her glass and twirled the long stem between her thumb and forefinger. 'A young woman, Joanna Alves. She was the sister of Professor Villanueva's secretary. Sister Mary Helen found her in the chapel — head bashed in.'

'Hot damn,' Jack swore softly. 'Any suspects?'

'Not really. Leonel da Silva is our best bet so far. At least he had motive and opportunity to kill the professor. He won't even deny he did it. But we don't have enough to charge him. So this morning he gets out, and this afternoon the Alves girl is dead.' Kate took another sip of her martini. 'And Sister Mary Helen may drive me bonkers.'

'How come?'

'She's got her mind made up he couldn't have done it.'

'Maybe she knows something you don't know.'

'No. I don't think so. It's her intuition. She says he has 'nice eyes.''

'Did you tell her about Baby-Face Nelson?'

'I was tempted to — but you know something, Jack?' Kate shrugged her shoulders. 'She's right.'

'Right?'

'He does have nice eyes. Something is bothering the guy for sure,' she said. 'Can't put my finger on it, but he just doesn't have the look of a murderer.'

Jack drained his glass. He was just about to launch into a firm, logical argument about the 'criminal look' being a fallacy, but he thought better of it. This was not at all the way he had planned the evening. Tonight he wanted romance, not logic. He decided to make the best of the situation. Maybe he could back into the proposal.

'That nun is sharp,' he said. 'Maybe she's right. Got the feeling she doesn't miss much.'

With the long glass rod, Jack restirred the pitcher of martinis. He topped Kate's glass and refilled his own. 'I wouldn't be surprised if she picked up something between you and me.'

Kate's mouth took on a straight-lipped fix. Jack recognized the fight sign. Go easy, he thought, lying back on the soft couch. Gently, he ran the heel of his hand up her rigid spine.

'Is that what this is all about?' Kate gestured toward the darkened living room.

'Meeting that nun yesterday made you feel guilty about us living together, so you are going to ask me to marry you? Again!'

'Yes and no,' Jack answered calmly.

'What do you mean — 'yes and no.''

'Yes, it is all about asking you to marry me, again.' Jack put special emphasis on the *again*. 'And no. No one made me feel guilty. I feel guilty all by myself. What I can never figure out is why the hell you don't.'

Kate stared indignantly. Jack met her stare. 'Do you know there is an official name for people like us?' She did not answer. 'It's POSSLQ: Persons of Opposite Sex Sharing Living Quarters.' He paused dramatically.

A smile played at the outer edges of Kate's tight lips. Humor was always the chink in her armor. Jack pressed his advantage. 'It's true,' he said. 'The Census Bureau invented the word. Do you want to go through life being my POSSLQ? On Valentine cards I can write 'Roses are red, Violets are blue. Will you be my POSSLQ'?'

Kate giggled. Relaxing, she kicked off her slippers and curled her legs up on the couch. Jack filled her empty glass. Snuggling closer to him, she began to twist a few strands of hair. Jack put his arm around her. Neither spoke for several moments.

Finally, Jack broke the silence. 'Kate, I love

you,' he said. 'You love me. Why not get married?' If he couldn't get her with romance, maybe he could do it with pure reason.

'Did your mother call again?'

'No,' he said, 'but even if she had, it's me who wants to marry you, not my mother.'

'I'm too tired to get into this tonight,' she said.

'That's an excuse.'

'Maybe. But I can't explain it. Maybe I'm not so sure myself. I know I love you. When and if I marry, there would be no one else I'd even consider.' She smiled at him.

Damn that melting smile, Jack thought, pulling her a little closer.

'I love my job,' she said. 'I worked to get where I am, and I do it as well as any man!'

'Some things you do much better,' he said, hoping to lighten her mood.

'I'm not kidding!'

'Maybe we could work something out.' The suggestion sounded feeble even to him.

'Maybe you could stay home and have the babies?' she said. Swinging her legs off the couch, Kate shoved her bare feet into her fuzzy blue bedroom slippers and pushed herself up off the couch.

No, this wasn't the way Jack had planned the evening at all. He'd give it one more try.

Reaching up, he caught her hips and pulled her on to his lap. He ran his hand down her thigh. 'That is a possibility we haven't considered.'

Turning toward him, Kate nestled comfortably into all his hollows. He could feel her body begin to relax. She fits perfectly, Jack thought, his arms enveloping her. I just can't let her go. He nuzzled his face into her fragrant hair. The blunt edges tickled his nose and chin.

'I love you,' he whispered.

'I love you, too,' she whispered back, 'and I can smell the rice burning.' Kate ran the tips of her fingers gently up the back of his neck.

Jack tingled all over. 'What the hell,' he said. 'Who likes rice, anyhow?'

Fifth Day

Sister Mary Helen woke up feeling furious. Morning Office in the Community Room did not help.

'I don't see why we can't pray in our own chapel.' Sister Therese's high-pitched whine before coffee made even placid Eileen flinch.

'Because the police have it cordoned off,' said Sister Anne, sitting cross-legged on the floor. Head bowed, she studied the tips of her toes wiggling in her doe-colored Paiutes.

'Well, I don't see why we couldn't stay in the back. This is the fifth day of my novena, and I'd like to say my prayers in the chapel. This place is certainly not conducive to my recollection,' Sister Therese said, taking in Sister Anne's lotus position.

'We can't go to the chapel because they are trying to find clues to the murderer,' Anne said. White-faced, she leaned back against the arm of the upholstered chair. She rested her hands on her knees and closed her eyes.

'Well, they certainly don't think one of us did it, do they?' Therese looked as though she had suddenly sniffed something sour. 'Really, it was a shame that it had to be one of us who found the body.' She rolled her eyes toward Mary Helen.

Mary Helen could feel both her eyebrows and her blood pressure rise. Fortunately, Eileen began intoning the Morning Office for the Dead.

After prayers, Eileen approached Mary Helen. 'You look like a thundercloud,' she said, as the two began the climb from the Sisters' Residence to the college dining room for breakfast. 'Were you able to sleep at all last night?'

'Not much. I just couldn't get yesterday off my mind. What's that line from Romeo and Juliet? 'Death lies on her like an untimely frost. Upon the sweetest flower of all the field'?'

Eileen put her hand on her friend's shoulder. Halfway up the hill, Mary Helen stopped to catch her breath. Ahead, slits of yellow light from the narrow windows pierced the dense morning fog. That same wet fog swallowed up the underbrush on the hillside and clung to the tips of the evergreens. The low moan of a foghorn floated in from the Gate.

'And what about you?' Mary Helen asked. 'Did you sleep?'

Eileen shook her head. 'I am still unable to believe it. And I can't seem to stop blubbering. It's like a horrid nightmare. The professor. Then Joanna. Poor, dear Marina!' She dug into her jacket pocket for a Kleenex.

Sister Anne, hands thrust deep into the pockets of her green corduroy car coat, caught up with the pair. She padded along beside Eileen. 'Hi, you two,' she said with forced cheerfulness. 'How are you doing?'

'Terrible,' Mary Helen snapped, suddenly annoyed. No one should be cheerful on a day like today. But one look at the young nun's face made Mary Helen regret her impatience. 'How about you?' she asked, softly.

'Terrible,' Anne answered, all pretense gone.

'I'll bet you are.' Vividly, Mary Helen recalled Anne and Inspector Gallagher leading Marina into the sacristy yesterday. The three of them had come through the back door. Marina's eyes were glazed, her slim body rigid. But she had insisted on seeing her sister's body. Softly, Marina had begun to whimper like a frightened, wounded animal. Then with one blood-curdling wail, she had shattered the silence. The shrill echo had filled the chapel and reverberated against the stained glass windows — like a moment frozen out of an Alfred Hitchcock film. Mary Helen had closed her eyes and covered her ears. 'Dear God, make all this go away,' she had prayed. But of course, nothing had gone away.

'I suppose you eventually got Marina to sleep?' Eileen said.

'You could call it that, I guess. The doctor finally had to give her a shot. I just came from checking on her. She's still out.'

Anne didn't look up, but continued to speak in a low, flat voice — as though she could hardly believe the reality of what had happened.

'What do I say when she wakes up?' Anne stopped and stared at the two older nuns. All the animation had left her face. Her lips formed a tight, straight line. Mary Helen had never seen that expression on Anne's face before. It took her only a moment to realize it was deep, unabated anger.

'What do I say to someone whose own sister, just a few days ago, was full of life and hope, and today, for no apparent reason, is a cold, mutilated corpse?' she asked, kicking a small, flat stone in the driveway. It bounced over the hillside and disappeared into the low, soupy fog. 'What do I say to someone who believes in God, trusts us, and whose sister has just been found murdered in our chapel?'

'Love, there's nothing to say,' Eileen answered quietly. 'There is just no way in the world to explain the mystery of evil.' The answer sounded so pat, so superficial, but unfortunately, so true.

'I know,' Anne said, 'but the whole thing makes me so damn mad!'

Mary Helen shared the emotion, although she might not have expressed it in exactly the same words.

As the three neared the rear door of the chapel, Mary Helen noticed a rough rope barring it. A sterile, black-and-white coroner's seal profaned the door. A small army of policemen in business suits had already invaded the peaceful campus. They swarmed everywhere — measuring, photographing, questioning. Mary Helen could feel her Irish blood begin to boil. Crazily, a favorite quote from *The Moonstone* jumped into her mind. 'Do you feel an uncomfortable heat in the pit of your stomach, Sir? And a nasty thumping at the top of your head? I call it detective fever.'

'Eileen. We have to do something about this!'

'About what, old dear — the mystery of evil, or about Anne's being angry?'

Mary Helen glared. Eileen shrugged. 'You needn't look at me like that. Those were the last two things I can remember being said. Which one is the antecedent of 'this'?'

'Neither. We must do something about

putting a stop to the murders on this campus.'

'And how, in God's name, would you suggest we do that?'

'By finding the murderer.' The dismal moan of a foghorn punctuated the last sentence.

'And just how do you propose we do that, when the entire San Francisco Police Department doesn't seem able to?'

'By investigating on our own. What do you think, Eileen?'

' "You may as well be hanged for a sheep as for a lamb," ' Eileen said.

Anne stopped to remove a small stone that had caught in the thong of her moccasin. 'Which reminds me,' she said, 'with all that happened yesterday afternoon, I never got a chance to tell you about the lists.'

'Lists?' The change of subject came too fast for Mary Helen.

'Yes. Remember, I asked Marina for a list of people Joanna interviewed? Well, I got it, plus the list the police asked for, the one of the people the professor had helped. I was going to give them to you, but then . . . ' Anne left her sentence unfinished.

Slowly, she rose and faced Mary Helen. 'I'll go to my office and get them, and you two can start with your investigating.'

'Not 'you two.' We three,' Mary Helen said. A determined dimple pitted each of her cheeks.

'You're really serious about this, aren't you? Why not leave it to the police?' Anne asked.

Detective fever would be too hard to explain. Mary Helen decided to get to the heart of the matter. 'Because I'm like you,' she said, 'and this whole murder business makes me so damn . . .' The word just shot out. But when it did, it tasted so good she said it again. 'This whole murder business makes me so damn mad!'

* * *

They were just finishing breakfast when Sister Therese whizzed by, brandishing the *Chronicle*. 'Look at this,' she said, pointing to the banner headlines. 'This paper is nothing but a scandal sheet.' She rolled her eyes toward Eileen, who, as librarian, always felt obliged to defend the printed word.

'No doubt about it, two murders at our college may be a scandal,' Eileen said, 'but no one can deny they are also news. And you must admit that's a nice picture of Cecilia.' Even she had to admit later, however, that HOMICIDE HITS HOLY

144

HILL in 72-point did smack a little of the sensational.

After Therese left, Mary Helen took her last swallow of coffee. 'Where are the lists?' she whispered.

'My office,' Anne whispered back.

'How about meeting there in twenty minutes?' Mary Helen looked at the other two. 'We can go over the lists and decide what to do.'

Both nuns nodded.

★ ★ ★

Anne put on the kettle for hot water, and the three were just settling around her large desk when the public address system clicked on. 'Sister Mary Helen, please report to the Sisters' Residence parlor, at once,' a tunnel voice announced.

'What now?' Mary Helen pushed away from the desk.

'Sister Mary Helen, please report to the Sisters' Residence parlor, at once,' the voice repeated, then added, 'Inspector Gallagher will meet you there.'

'Oh, oh,' Anne said. 'Do you think he knows about our getting these lists?' She shoved the papers toward the middle of the desk.

'Don't be silly,' Mary Helen said. 'How could he?'

'Shouldn't we tell the police we want to help?'

'Why bother them with it?' Mary Helen asked, fooling not even herself. 'We are doing nothing wrong. We are simply interested citizens helping our police force. It's the decent thing to do. After all, it is our duty. Why, Inspector Gallagher will be grateful.'

'Good night, nurse, Mary Helen,' Eileen said. 'You had better stop before you begin to believe it yourself.'

'Don't you think I'm right?' Mary Helen turned toward Eileen.

'Old dear, you don't want to know what I think,' Eileen said, then added, smiling, 'what is it you want us to do while you're gone?'

'Why don't you go through the lists? Maybe pick out the names that appear on both papers. We can start to call those people.'

Mary Helen left the two huddled over the desk.

★ ★ ★

Mary Helen walked quickly down the driveway toward the Sisters' Residence. She hugged the right edge of the road, leaving the student drivers enough room to speed up the hill. No sense being run down by a ten o'clock scholar, she thought, watching out for the few cars racing up the hill.

She stopped for a moment to admire the formal gardens. The primroses spread an elegant apron of color in front of the main building. They look so perky and well-mannered, she thought; in fact, the whole campus looked so stately and safe it was hard to believe what had happened here. An unmarked police car swished by. The grim faces of the two officers brought her back to reality.

* * *

Both Inspectors Gallagher and Murphy were waiting in the parlor when the old nun arrived. Kate smiled warmly when she saw Mary Helen. 'Sit down, Sister,' she said, motioning toward an overstuffed chair.

Gallagher squirmed. He seemed too big for the tiny parlor. Finally, he perched on the edge of a straight-backed mahogany chair. 'We'd like to ask you a few more questions, Sister,' he said.

'I think I told you everything I know last night,' Mary Helen said, remembering her hour-long session in the sacristy.

'There's one thing we wondered about.' Kate took out her narrow note pad. 'When you reported the body, why didn't you tell us who it was?'

'I wasn't really sure,' Mary Helen answered.

'You weren't sure?' Kate interrupted. 'You mean you had never seen the girl before?'

'Not exactly. I saw her once over the side of the hill. She looked like Marina, and so I asked Eileen who she was.'

'Over the side of what hill?'

Reluctantly, Mary Helen explained her special spot to Kate. She thought she glimpsed a look of camaraderie cross the young woman's face when she mentioned her addiction to 'whodunits.'

Why not? Hadn't she heard that it was a notorious fact that detective stories were the favorite reading of statesmen and college presidents? Why not police inspectors?

'I saw her with Tony, the gardener.'

'What were they doing?' Kate looked up from her notes.

'Kissing — but in my opinion, not too affectionately.'

Gallagher cleared his throat. 'Could you explain what you mean, Sister?'

'Yes, Inspector. Tony grabbed her and gave her a very rough kiss. It didn't look much like love to me. And by the time you are my age,

148

you begin to recognize love when you see it.'

Kate changed the subject. 'What did you tell me you were doing just before you found the body?' she asked.

Gallagher turned and frowned at Kate. Mary Helen couldn't tell if he was surprised or frustrated. In either case, she didn't blame him. Tony the gardener seemed like an excellent choice of suspect to her. For a moment, she wondered why Kate didn't pursue the subject. Then it dawned on her. Of course! She had struck a chord. Kate suspected that she had picked up the chemistry between Jack and her. Well, she had.

'What were you doing just before you found the body?' Kate repeated. Her eyes avoided Mary Helen's.

'I told you. I was looking up Dom Sebastiao in the library.'

'How did you happen to know that the statue was Dom Sebastiao?'

'Leonel told me.' As soon as she mentioned Leonel, Mary Helen knew she had made a mistake. Kate looked up from her notes.

Gallagher rose. Putting his foot on the chair, he bent forward, and his face came close to Mary Helen's. 'When did he tell you about the statue, Sister?'

Sister Mary Helen resisted the temptation

to tell him to get his foot off the good mahogany chair. 'The day after the professor's . . . ' She hesitated a moment, recalling the scene in the man's office.

'Skull was bashed in?' Gallagher's finished the sentence. 'Just like that young girl you found last night?' He took his foot off the chair.

In her mind's eye, Mary Helen saw the professor again, his cold face wreathed in an ever-widening halo of red. Then, Joanna, legs dangling, her delicate features splattered with dried blood. Both skulls crushed. Were they both killed with a statue? Could Leonel have done it? Was that what Gallagher was getting at? Mary Helen put her hand over her mouth, fighting nausea.

'Sister, are you okay?' Kate slid her arm around the nun's shoulder. Mary Helen didn't trust herself to speak. She simply nodded.

'We're finished for now,' Kate assured her. 'You may go. We'll get in touch with you again, if we need you.'

Stiffly, Mary Helen rose from the chair. Forcing a smile, she bowed toward the two inspectors. Silently, she left the parlor.

'Poor gal,' Kate's voice floated down the hall behind her. 'You've got to admit, Denny, she's feisty, but she's got plenty of heart.'

'Not the best quality for police work.' Gallagher tried hard to sound tough.

'But top-notch for a nun,' Kate said.

★　★　★

By the time Sister Mary Helen returned to Anne's office, the college bell was tolling noon. After a quick lunch, the three nuns met again, huddling in the small basement office with door closed, candles lit. Mary Helen's spirits rose.

'We look for all the world like a scene from the French underground,' Eileen whispered. She snatched the thought right out of Mary Helen's mind. Anne bit her lower lip.

'This is a wonderful list!' Mary Helen scanned the sheets of paper Eileen handed her.

'The professor didn't have many on his,' Eileen said, running her finger down the first nine names.

'That's all he helped?' Mary Helen asked. 'Maybe he wasn't such a philanthropist, after all.'

'The poor devil really wasn't here very long.' Mary Helen could have counted on Eileen to defend him. Eileen didn't believe in speaking ill of the dead.

'But he was the head of the department?'

'Actually, we had a terrible upset in the history department several years ago, and had to get in several new people. Villanueva came highly recommended, as I understand it.'

'Then, he wasn't someone who had worked himself up through the ranks?'

'Not at all.'

'Interesting!' Mary Helen said.

'What do you mean by 'interesting'?'

'I don't know, but that's what Kate Murphy said when I finished my statement last night, and as long as we are into investigating . . . '

Anne's giggle filled the small office. Quickly, she made a cup of tea and two cups of instant coffee. 'Let's get back to the list,' she said, setting the mugs on the desk.

'Well, Professor Villanueva's nine people were on Joanna's list,' Eileen continued. 'Then she had another maybe two hundred or so of her own.'

'Now you know as well as I we couldn't possibly call all those people,' Eileen said, not stopping for breath. 'Anne and I were just wondering what to do when I suddenly noticed a small dot by some of the names.' She shoved the papers toward Mary Helen.

Good old Eileen, Mary Helen thought, adjusting her bifocals. Who else would notice a speck that size? All that dusting had come in handy.

'How many with dots?' Mary Helen asked.

'About thirty.'

'Plus the professor's nine makes thirty-nine. Divided by three equals thirteen phone calls each.'

'Good God, Mary Helen!' Eileen's eyebrows shot up. 'Don't we have enough trouble without putting thirteen anything on a list? I divided the thirty-nine into three lists, all right. Two have twelve names; one has fifteen.'

'Who gets the fifteen?'

'You do. This investigating business was your idea.'

'We put Kevin Doherty on your list,' Anne said. 'I got his phone number from Marina.' She slipped a small piece of scratch paper toward Mary Helen.

Mary Helen had almost forgotten about Kevin Doherty, the young man Joanna had met at the University of San Francisco. The plot was thickening. Had Joanna been with Kevin before she died?

Mary Helen shoved the scrap of paper into her pocket. 'Now for the phones,' she said.

'Well, Anne has one here. I have one in my library office and, Mary Helen, you can use the one in the convent.' Eileen had obviously thought the whole thing through.

'Wait a minute, you two,' Anne said, as the

older sisters stood to leave. 'What am I supposed to say when I get these people?' Apparently, Anne was going along with the idea, but had not yet caught the spirit of the hunt.

'Just ask them about Joanna. When was the last time they saw her — if they knew the professor, et cetera. Play it by ear.'

'You'll do fine, love. Don't worry.' Eileen patted her hand.

'I have this awful feeling we shouldn't be doing this,' Anne said.

'Nonsense,' Mary Helen said. 'We owe it to our college.' At least that's my press statement if we get caught, she thought, shifting her eyes from Anne's. 'When should we meet back here? Two hours?'

'If you say let's synchronize our watches, I'll turn up my toes!' Eileen's face wrinkled into a grin.

$$\star \quad \star \quad \star$$

As Sister Mary Helen headed back down the hill toward the convent, she suddenly realized the morning fog had burned off. Completely! Sun flooded the campus. 'Shook foil.' The words from Hopkins's poem flitted through her mind. What was the rest? 'The world is charged with the grandeur of God. It will flame out, like shining from shook foil.'

The campus and the city below it sparkled under the crisp autumn sun like 'shining from shook foil.' How in the world did the poem end? She hadn't thought of it in years. 'The Holy Ghost over the bent World broods with warm breast and ah! bright wings.'

In the sun's warmth she felt His wings brooding over her, His warm breast. Yes, this murder business would, indeed, have a bright ending. 'And if You have half a chance, God,' she prayed earnestly, 'please, end it quickly.'

★　★　★

Just before four o'clock, the three nuns reconvened in Anne's office, their lists marked and dog-eared.

'Well, how did we do?' Mary Helen asked brightly.

Anne had sunk into an overstuffed pillow. Slowly, she was easing her legs into a lotus position. Her list lay curled on the floor in front of her. Eileen looked peaked. Too much smiling, Mary Helen thought. Eileen was the only person she knew who smiled when she talked on the phone. As a matter of fact, Eileen's was the only face she remembered that ever looked tired from smiling.

Eileen's list was spread out neatly on the

155

desk. 'I had both Luis and Leonel on my list,' she said. 'No sense in calling either of them. I can talk to them both up here. Furthermore, I should let poor Leonel rest. I'm sure he's had quite enough questions from the police. I couldn't get any of the others from the professor's list. For the rest, I got nowhere in a terrible hurry. Some of them knew our professor. Of course, everyone knew Joanna. But no one knew where she had been recently. Quite frankly,' she said, 'my phoning was a dismal failure.'

'How about you? Mary Helen looked toward Anne, who, eyes closed, was rolling her head counterclockwise. 'Are you all right?' the old nun asked.

'Fine. Just relaxing my neck muscles.' Mary Helen thought she heard Anne's neck crack.

'I also drew blanks,' Anne said, 'except for one. A Mrs Rubiero. Professor Villanueva helped her two nephews to emigrate. They lived with her after they arrived. Well, she hasn't heard from them for a while, and she's a bit concerned. I couldn't tell why, however.'

'What do you mean, you couldn't tell why?'

'I couldn't tell if she thinks something happened to them, or if she thinks they're 'flaky,' and that's what's upsetting her. I made an appointment for you to see her on Saturday.'

'Why me?'

'Because youth appeals to youth, and I figured the opposite might also hold.' Anne opened one eye to check Mary Helen's reaction.

The older nun chose to ignore the remark. She simply said, 'Fine.'

'And you, old dear? Did you get anywhere at all?' Eileen asked.

'Not too far,' Mary Helen said, 'but I did pick up a tone in several voices.'

'A tone?'

'Yes, I think something is going on. When I mentioned Professor Villanueva, several of the older folks acted as if they suspected something they were not willing to tell. One woman said she was worried about the young people the man had helped. Do you know what she did when I asked her why?'

'What?'

'She hung up!' Mary Helen let that sink in before she played her trump card. 'Do you know whom I did get?' she asked.

'Who?'

'Kevin Doherty! I hit the jackpot with him. He's been worried about Joanna since she finished her thesis. Wants to talk about it. I have an appointment with him at ten o'clock tomorrow morning, here.'

Mary Helen checked her watch. 'It's almost

dinner time. Let's split up and come to the dining room from different angles,' she said. 'And don't be late. People might wonder what we've been up to.'

'They'd never guess,' Anne said, without opening her eyes.

Mary Helen pushed all the sheets of paper toward Eileen. 'You keep these someplace. Maybe locked in your office. Someplace where no one can get at them.'

Eileen nodded. 'And if someone questions me, old dear, do you have a cyanide capsule you'd like me to slip under my tongue?'

★ ★ ★

Head down, Mary Helen rushed along the dim corridor toward the dining room. The loose tiles clicked to the steady rhythm of her footsteps. She didn't even notice Kate Murphy coming toward her.

'Sister, may I talk to you a minute?' The voice startled her. Kate must have been with the investigating team in the chapel.

'Surely,' Mary Helen said, without looking up.

Taking the old nun by the elbow, Kate steered her into a small hopper room off the hall. 'It will only take a minute,' she said.

Even before turning to face Kate, Mary

Helen had begun to examine her own conscience. There were only a few things she could think of right off to feel guilty about. Had Kate discovered the broken seal on the professor's office door, or was it the lists, or the phone calling? Had she realized the three nuns had begun their own investigation?

'This is a little embarrassing,' Kate started, 'but I'd like to ask you a personal question, if I may.'

A cold wash of relief swept over Mary Helen.

'When I went to school here,' Kate said, 'the older nuns, in fact, all the nuns, were a bit more . . . ' Kate stumbled for a word.

'Traditional?' Mary Helen supplied.

'Right. And I always thought the older women might stick with that.'

'They might.'

'Well, if I may ask.' Embarrassed Kate cleared her throat. 'Why didn't you?'

Mary Helen smiled. She remembered distinctly the shocked looks of her peers when, after forty years in the traditional habit of her Order, she had decided to change to modern dress.

At first, her hairdo had given her a little trouble. But a hairdresser friend had rescued her with a short feather cut and a permanent. The result startled her the first few times she passed a mirror. Now she found her hair neat and easy to manage.

Smiling, she gave Kate the same answer she had given to many of her contemporaries who resisted the updating of the Order. 'Well, I figured life would go on with or without me,' she said, 'so I might as well go with it. I must admit that I did resist one change.'

'What was that?'

'I refused to change my name! When I received the habit,' she said, 'I was given the name Mary Helen. I have lived with it so long I think of myself as Mary Helen.'

Kate nodded. 'That seems valid,' she said.

'When we had a choice to return to our baptismal names, I refused. Long ago, I had stopped thinking of myself as Sally O'Connor.' The old nun bent toward Kate. 'Besides,' she whispered, 'a seventy-five-year-old Sister Sally sounds ridiculous!' Kate's laughter filled the small hopper room.

'Sister,' she asked, 'would it ever be possible for you to come to my home for dinner?'

'It would be my pleasure,' Mary Helen answered.

'Good.' Kate took the nun's hand and pressed it, giving an extra squeeze before she hurried down the corridor.

Puzzled, Mary Helen watched her go.

160

Something was odd. Why in the world did Kate Murphy want her to come to dinner? Why did she seem so eager to get to know her better? Did Kate suspect that she, too, was investigating? Maybe she wanted to collaborate. Mary Helen allowed herself a moment to fantasize before logic took over. More likely, it had something to do with that tall, black-haired inspector, Jack Bassetti. Yes, she'd put her money on Jack Bassetti.

★ ★ ★

After dinner, most of the nuns crowded into the television room for the local news. All eyes were eagerly glued to the large console as Sister Anne tuned it in. They were not disappointed. The two murders at Mount St Francis College for Women filled the lead segment.

A brash woman reporter shoved a microphone in front of Sister Cecilia. 'How did you feel, Sister, when a second body was discovered at your college?' she asked.

From the look on Cecilia's face, Mary Helen thought, the answer was clear.

'And so far the killer has not been apprehended,' the anchorman pontificated. 'Will homicide hit the Holy Hill, again?' he asked, leaving a pregnant pause. Fadeout.

'Mother of God!' Sister Therese's ejaculation whipped across the hush. Quickly, she left her place to recheck the window latches. They could hear her patter down the corridor to set the dead bolt on the front door.

'I can't stand this,' Mary Helen mouthed to Eileen. 'If we don't do something, we'll spend the entire evening listening for someone approaching to murder us in our beds.'

Eileen grimaced. 'Why don't we play a fast game of pinochle?' she asked. 'We could give a semblance of normalcy, anyway.'

'Good idea,' Mary Helen said, grabbing Anne and a fourth.

As hard as she tried, Mary Helen couldn't keep her mind on the game. Even Eileen frowned once, when she led with the wrong trump. Finally, Mary Helen threw in the last trick. She yawned. 'I'm sorry,' she said, 'I know I'm distracted and playing poorly. Right now, I think my best move would be to go straight to bed.' She was a little annoyed when no one, not even pleasant Eileen, had the courtesy to contradict her.

★   ★   ★

Mary Helen drew a warm bath. She threw in a bit of bath oil in the hope it would help relax her. After soaking until her fingers were prunelike, she hopped into bed, wide awake. She tried reading for a few minutes, but she couldn't concentrate on the plot.

Finally, in desperation, she switched off the bedroom light and stared at the ceiling. The floodlights floated eerie, green shadows across the flat white. Mary Helen's mind whirled. Was Leonel the murderer, after all? she wondered. Or was it that mysterious presence she had sensed in the hallway the night the professor died? Was it someone she knew, or a total stranger? And Joanna. Who had killed Joanna? Had her murderer still been in the chapel when she'd discovered the body? She hadn't thought of that before. He could have been crouched down in a pew just waiting to pounce. And was she sure it was a *he*? Could the murderer by any chance be a *she*? But who? Where was the murderer now? Home asleep? Do murderers sleep well at night? Or was he out roaming around? Maybe even stalking the darkened campus. Mary Helen flipped on the bedroom lamp. Grabbing her glasses from the night stand, she checked to make sure she had locked the door. The button was pushed in. She flicked off the lamp. What would Kevin Doherty have to say in the morning?

Get hold of yourself, old girl, she thought, deliberately forcing her mind to let go. Think of something else. For example, why did you lose so badly at pinochle tonight? She replayed her hand, but before she took the final trick, she fell into a fitful sleep.

The Jack of Diamonds was chasing the Queen of Spades down the long, narrow corridors of the main building. Whenever he gained on her, she would lash at him with the yellow flower in her right hand. In a fit of rage, the Jack pursued her into the chapel. He cornered her in the front pew, just before the altar. She cowered before him. Raising his thick arm high above her head, he brandished not his usual wide sword, but a bloodied statue of Dom Sebastiao. Again and again, he pommeled her thin body until the Queen of Spades lay a broken heap at his feet.

Sixth Day

Sister Mary Helen unbolted the heavy front door of the convent. Again! It was the third time she had done it in less than twenty minutes. This time she stationed herself in the small front parlor to stake out the door. Who was the culprit, the phantom bolter who kept slipping in to relock it? She had her suspicions.

The sound of quick, nervous footsteps pattering down the long corridor confirmed them. Shoving her bifocals up the bridge of her nose, she confronted Sister Therese in the tiny entrance hall.

'Why do you keep rebolting the door?' she asked, trying not to sound too piqued.

'Because you never know who could walk right in here and murder one of us in our own convent.'

'In broad daylight?'

'The Alves girl was murdered in broad daylight.'

Therese had a point, one that could hardly be refuted. Mary Helen changed to a more positive subject. 'How's your novena coming?' she asked.

'Just fine. I'm on the sixth day. We should be getting some results very soon,' Therese said with such confidence that Mary Helen didn't doubt for one moment that she was right.

'And if the point you are trying to make is that I should rely on prayer alone and not bolt the door, you are sadly mistaken.' Her small, sharp nose lifted. 'God helps those who help themselves,' she said, quoting the old proverb as though it were Holy Writ.

Mary Helen watched the small, birdlike figure stomp down the hallway. Therese had misunderstood. Mary Helen's point was a simple one. Kevin Doherty was scheduled to arrive any minute now, and she pulled back the bolt so that the convent wouldn't sound like a fortress when she opened the door for him. She realized, however, that any explanation would be lost on Therese's fleeing back. The soft chime of the doorbell broke into her thoughts.

'Good morning,' Sister Mary Helen said, opening the door wide. A tall, lanky young man stood in the doorway. He looked as if he should be suited up and dribbling a basketball.

'I'm Kevin Doherty,' he said. 'I've an appointment with . . . ' He hesitated, searching for the name.

'With me. Come in, please.' Mary Helen led the young man to a small side parlor. He dropped into a chair. Self-consciously, he tried to ease his long legs into a comfortable position. It took three before he settled on putting them straight out in front of him.

Sitting opposite him, watching him fidget, Mary Helen realized what a striking couple the two must have made. Kevin, with his full head of golden hair, pug-nosed, a real Celt; Joanna, blue-black haired, delicate featured, a Latin beauty. 'Star-crossed lovers,' she and Shakespeare would have agreed.

'So nice of you to come over, Kevin,' Mary Helen began, attempting to put the young man at ease. It had always been her contention that sitting in state in a small, sterile convent parlor could make the most phlegmatic person tense.

'My pleasure, Sister.' She could see his Adam's apple move up and down his thin neck. He was having trouble getting the words out. 'I — I really . . . ' he stammered, then swallowed hard. 'I really care about Joanna. I'd like . . . to help.'

'Perhaps if you could tell me a little about her,' Mary Helen said gently. 'How you met. Where she might have been the past few days. Whatever you think could be important.'

Doherty pulled his legs in and hunched

forward. He looked to Sister Mary Helen, for all the world like a curly-haired, freckled-faced *Thinker*.

'Well, we met in class,' he said. 'Went out a few times, and I think we would have had something going if it hadn't been for this thesis business.'

'What thesis business?'

'She got really involved. Something she discovered in her research.'

'Do you know what it was?' Mary Helen's heart began to beat faster. Maybe, at last, she was hitting on something. Maybe Therese's novena was beginning to pay off.

'No,' he said.

Her heart dropped. 'Just *no*?'

'She wouldn't tell me what it was all about. Said it was dangerous. Didn't want me to know.' The young man shrugged his shoulders. 'Can you imagine that, Sister? Too dangerous for a guy my size, but okay for a little thing like her.' It seemed incredible to the old nun, too.

'The whole business became almost an — an obsession,' he said. 'Worried me a lot.' He cracked his knuckles and shook his head sadly. 'I guess I was right to worry. Like she said, it was dangerous. I still can't believe . . . ' He stopped, tears glistening in his eyes. Mary Helen resisted the urge to put her arms around him.

'Do you think she suffered much?' he asked, after a long pause.

'I don't think so.' Mary Helen shuddered, remembering the girl's crushed skull. 'I think death was quick.'

'I'd like to find the guy who did it and break him in two.' Doherty cracked his knuckles again.

'Even if you don't break him in two, it's important we find the fellow,' Mary Helen agreed, 'so that he won't harm anyone else.' She paused a moment to let that sink in. 'Now tell me, Kevin, is there anything at all you can remember about the research?'

He leaned back in his chair and wiped his eyes with the back of his hands. 'Well, I know it was on the Portuguese immigrants. Some kind of an abuse, I think. She went down to Santa Clara County a lot, talking to people.'

'Can you remember any names she may have mentioned?'

'Yeah, once,' he said. 'Mrs Rubiero.'

Rubiero — that was the woman Anne had made the appointment with. Maybe they were getting someplace, after all. 'Why do you remember that name?'

Kevin shrugged. 'No reason,' he said, 'except that I met Joanna that night for dinner in Millbrae. She had just come from

Mrs Rubiero's. She mentioned it, and the name stuck with me because we had a Portuguese kid on my high school basketball team by the same name.'

He thought for a moment. 'You know what, Sister? Now that I think about it, it was right after that that she started to get funny.'

'Funny?'

'Yeah. Broke dates. Wouldn't talk much. Didn't have time for me. I could never figure out why. She said it would all be different when something got straightened out.'

'Maybe she'd found another boyfriend.' Mary Helen said that as gently as she could, remembering the scene with Tony on the hillside.

'Naw,' the young man said, with a masculine ego that Mary Helen found amusing. 'She really liked me.'

'Did she ever mention a young man named Tony?' she asked.

'That weirdo! Yeah, she mentioned him plenty. Hated him. She'd go the other way if she saw him coming. He even tried to bother her once or twice when I was with her.'

So she had been correct about the kiss. It had not been too affectionate. She stored that information on the back burner of her mind.

'You don't think that guy had anything to do with Joanna's ... ' Doherty seemed unable to say the word 'murder'. 'Why, if he touched her, I'll break the little bastard in two with my bare hands.' He slammed his clenched fist against the arm of the chair.

Mary Helen jumped. All the color had left the boy's face. Only the blotchy freckles stood out; those, and the blazing blue eyes. Talk about your wild Irish temper, Mary Helen thought, studying the young man. She cleared her throat. 'Kevin, I know you are upset,' she said. 'And you have every right to be,' she added quickly.

'Sister, do you think he did it?' He strained the question through his teeth.

'I don't know what to think,' she answered honestly. The young gardener was on her list to call. She'd put him off till later. She'd have to get to him today or tomorrow.

'If he did it, I'll kill him.' Doherty's bellow interrupted her thought.

'For heaven's sake, Kevin, haven't we had enough killing?' she asked in her sternest, schoolmarm voice. 'Why don't we try to make sure no one else has to feel as hurt and angry as you do today?' She stopped, surprised at her own impatience.

For a moment the young man stared at her. He reminded her of a valiant warrior who has suddenly lost his taste for the battle. Unexpectedly, he hunched forward, burying

171

his face in his two broad hands. Mary Helen felt a hot, sick pain of empathy. Reaching over, she tousled his blond, curly head. 'I'm so sorry,' she said.

Then, like the tall, lanky youngster he was, Kevin Doherty sobbed unashamedly.

When he looked up, his freckled face was streaked with tears. 'I think I loved her, Sister,' he said, cracking his knuckles.

'I think you did,' Mary Helen answered.

★ ★ ★

On her way to lunch, Mary Helen met Eileen. 'Feel like a stretch before we eat?' she asked.

'It sounds marvelous.' Eileen checked her watch. 'More than likely, there'll be a line in the dining room if we go now. Ten minutes of fresh air will do us a world of good.'

'Up this way and back?' Mary Helen asked, swerving on to the narrow path leading off the driveway. Eileen followed. The two walked in silence for several yards.

'Why so quiet?' Mary Helen said finally.

'At this pace, old dear, who can both talk and breathe?'

Mary Helen slowed down. 'I saw Kevin Doherty this morning,' she said. 'Poor kid. Really loved Joanna.'

Eileen clucked sympathetically. 'Did he say anything you think might be helpful?'

'I don't know. He talked about the thesis.'

'The missing thesis?'

'Yes, I'm sure there is some connection. He also asked me if I thought Tony might have done it.'

Eileen looked shocked. 'Tony kill Joanna? Why, that seems impossible. Tony's a gardener! He spends so much time making things grow and flourish, I just can't imagine him killing anything, much less anybody. Besides, wasn't he a bit sweet on Joanna?' Without waiting for an answer, Eileen continued. 'No,' she said, shaking her head for emphasis. 'I just can't believe it. Love and a garden — that should add up to something good, not evil.' She stopped, a sudden look of realization in her wide, gray eyes. 'Although I must admit it didn't work out quite so well in the garden of Eden, now did it?'

Mary Helen knew a rhetorical question when she heard one. 'Who loves a garden, still his Eden keeps,' she quoted, hoping to ease Eileen's mind a bit.

Her friend kicked a loose pebble in the pathway. 'What do you think?'

'Tony's on my list to call.'

'Not about Tony — about the whole business.'

173

'I don't know what to think until I mull it over for a while,' Mary Helen answered. The two walked a few more feet. 'You know, I've done an awful lot of mulling about these murders,' she said.

'And just who hasn't, old dear?'

'I really can't figure out yet how the professor and Leonel and Marina and Joanna and now Tony, plus a missing thesis, figure into this puzzle, but I'm sure they do. One thought that has struck me is that whoever our murderer is, he or she always makes very sure poor Leonel is around so he can be implicated.'

'Unless poor Leonel is our murderer,' Eileen reminded her softly.

Mary Helen continued as though she hadn't heard the remark. 'Now it is our job to figure out just who could possibly know all of Leonel's movements.' She stopped and faced Eileen.

'Why, several people could, I'm sure.'

'Who comes to your mind first?'

'Marina, of course, but . . . ' Her gray eyes opened wide, then blinked. 'But you couldn't possibly think . . . '

'He was so defensive about her at the Hall of Justice. Remember?'

'Certainly I remember. But you can't possibly believe for one moment that sweet, young Marina killed the professor and then her own sister.'

'Why can't I possibly believe it?'

'Let's turn back.' Eileen checked her watch. 'If we don't hurry, we'll miss lunch completely,' she said, walking quickly toward the driveway. Obviously, Eileen didn't want to discuss the subject any further.

'I said, why can't I possibly believe it?' Mary Helen pushed the point.

'You can't believe it because it's . . . it's so unnatural,' Eileen stammered. 'Whoever heard of such a thing?'

'Really, it's nothing so new,' Mary Helen said, following close behind her friend. 'You just mentioned the Garden of Eden. And you know as well as I do, that if you keep on reading the Genesis story, the next thing you run right into is the story of Cain and Abel.'

Turning quickly on her heel, Eileen shot her old friend what she later denied was a dirty look.

★ ★ ★

'Damn!' Kate Murphy slammed down the phone receiver. The creeping charlie in her desk planter quivered.

Across from her, Gallagher looked up. 'What the hell is wrong with you?' he asked in a mild, controlled voice.

'For God's sake, Denny, don't use that tone of voice on me. It makes me feel like a — an hysterical woman.' Replacing her earring, she stared out the window of the Hall of Justice at the heavy freeway traffic.

'Well?' Gallagher returned to the large stack of papers piled on his desk.

'Just what did that 'well' mean?'

'It could mean 'well, what the hell is wrong with you?' or it could mean 'well, you are a — an'' — he mimicked her fumble for the correct article — ''an hysterical woman!''

Kate knew that much.

'You wanted to be the detective, Murphy; you figure it out,' he said, going back to his paper work.

Kate felt the color rise in her face. She flopped into her swivel chair and began to twist a few strands of hair around her index finger. 'Sorry, Denny,' she said. 'I'm just frustrated, that's all. I didn't mean to take it out on you.'

'Let's start again. What the hell is wrong with you?'

'It's that damn nun!' Kate slammed her fist on her desk.

'Hey, Murphy, no police brutality,' one of the officers hollered from the coffee urn. Chauvinistic smart-asses, she thought, I'll

176

show them when I catch the Holy Hill killer!

'The problem?' Gallagher asked.

'The names of the people the professor helped — the ones I got from Marina. I couldn't get hold of a single one of them. I called Marina at home and got the names of any of their relatives that she knew. I've been calling them. Most every call ends the same way. 'The Seester, she ask already,' they say. When I mention I'm from the police, they hang up. What I can't figure out is where 'Seester' got the list, and why in the hell she's calling these people.'

'Why do you want to make her stop?' Gallagher asked.

'Well, for starters, it is police business. And, for finishers, if she does happen to run into a serious lead, we could have another murder on our hands.'

'Then tell her.' Gallagher made it sound so simple.

'What do I do? Go up to the college, flash my badge, and tell the old lady, 'Bug off, Sister'.'

'Back at St Anne's, one old gal, Sister Felicia, used to drive the pastor, Father Hennessey, bananas. He could control the police and the politicians in the City, but he couldn't begin to be a match for Felicia. Well, one day they must have had an awful

Donnybrook. Old Hennessey said to me, 'Denny, nuns are like bees. Leave 'em alone and they make honey. Interfere, and you'll always get stung.' I was just a kid, but I never forgot it.'

'The point, Denny — what is the point?'

Gallagher leaned back in his swivel chair. He studied her with what Kate was sure could be classified as a supercilious grin. 'Well,' he said, 'as the old saying goes, Katie girl, if you can't lick 'em, join 'em.'

★ ★ ★

It took no longer than twenty minutes for Kate Murphy to arrive at the Sisters' Residence. And it didn't take her more than another ten minutes to outline, politely but very definitely, that criminal investigation was her domain; hers, and the SFPD's. She also enumerated the many dangers inherent in amateurs meddling in murder cases, not the least of which was being murdered themselves.

She's not a redhead for nothing, Mary Helen thought, watching Kate sitting on the edge of the parlor chair. She waited, silently, until she felt sure Kate had finished her well-prepared speech. The old nun tried to look concerned and contrite.

178

'Aren't you curious about where we got the list?' she asked meekly.

'At the moment, I'm more curious about why you feel you should get involved in a police investigation,' Kate said.

Sister Mary Helen outlined as succinctly as she could the deep anger and resentment she felt about a murderer being allowed to terrorize the college. She thought about using 'damn mad' for emphasis, but then decided she'd save that until she knew Kate a little better. The young woman remained silent. Mary Helen hurried on to her positive intuition about Leonel's being not only innocent, but victimized. Kate opened her mouth, but, thankfully, closed it again. Mary Helen was sure that line from Shakespeare, 'I have no other but a woman's reason: I think him so, because I think him so,' would not fit into Kate's idea of a well-orchestrated homicide investigation. She felt she knew the young woman that well.

'Now, are you curious about the list?' Mary Helen asked when she finally finished what she later described to Eileen as her *Apologia pro culpa Helenae*.

Exhausted, Kate lit a cigarette, inhaled deeply, and sank back into the chair. 'Frankly, yes,' she said.

'I discovered Joanna had written a thesis on

the Portuguese immigrants,' she said, 'which disappeared from Sister Eileen's library at just about the same time that Joanna did. Now, I call that too much of a coincidence. Don't you?'

'I guess I might have, if I had known it!' Mary Helen thought Kate still sounded a little annoyed. She hurried on.

'I just thought to myself — Portuguese-thesis-professor-Joanna. There has to be some connection. But the thesis was missing, and the professor's office was sealed.' She hurried over that. 'So we couldn't get in for a duplicate copy. Anyway, we . . . '

'Who's we?' Kate asked, too quietly.

'Sister Eileen, Sister Anne, and I,' the old nun answered.

Kate groaned. 'That's how you got to all those people so quickly. 'Seester called.' There were three 'seesters' calling.'

Mary Helen ignored the interruption. 'Anyway, we got the list from Marina of the people Joanna had interviewed for her thesis. It was a very long one, but Eileen found dots by some of the names.'

'Dots?' Kate took a final drag of her cigarette and stubbed it out.

'Right. We figured those dots must have some significance, so we divided it into three. Plus, Joanna had a boyfriend, Kevin Doherty, whom I talked to this morning.'

'What did he say?'

'He said, among other things, that she got funny after she talked to Mrs Rubiero.'

'Who?'

'Rubiero. She has relatives Professor Villanueva helped. She's on the list. In fact, I've an appointment with her tomorrow, if you'd like to go along.'

'If I'm not intruding.' Kate sounded a bit sarcastic to Sister Mary Helen, who wasn't sure if being sarcastic was better or worse than being annoyed.

'What did the boyfriend mean by 'funny'?' Kate lit another cigarette, took a long drag, and exhaled.

The old nun opened the long, narrow, parlor window, hoping the smell of smoke wouldn't cling to her clothes.

'He said she became obsessed with her research. Something she needed to solve. Lost interest in him.'

'Maybe it was another boy. That Tony you mentioned?'

'I suggested that, but Kevin said she hated him. He got very upset about Tony. You don't suppose Tony might have something to do with the murders?'

'Not a chance. I checked his alibi for the night Villanueva was murdered. He was in a bar in Santa Clara. Dozens of witnesses. Even the bartender remembers him.'

Mary Helen felt slightly disappointed. If Tony had had no alibi, then he might be guilty, and this whole awful mess would be solved. Suddenly, she felt her face flush. Poor Tony. Why, that wasn't even cricket. The poor devil was probably every bit as innocent as Leonel — or almost.

'And the people you called, what did you ask them?' Kate continued. Apparently, she hadn't noticed Mary Helen's flush.

'We asked about Joanna. How well they knew her. When they saw her last. Anything they could remember about the questions she'd asked them. Did they know the professor, too? All the usual questions.'

'What do you mean 'usual questions'?' Kate asked, a faint smile playing on the corners of her wide mouth.

Mary Helen could feel her face redden again. She squirmed. For a moment she felt a little like Mrs Pollifax. It was not a pleasant feeling, since she had always considered Mrs Pollifax a bit of an eccentric. 'You know, the ones all detectives ask,' she said, as nonchalantly as she could.

'And the answers?'

'Although they were all very polite, for the most part we drew blanks,' she said. 'But I

182

have some suspicions.'

'Oh?'

Kate glanced at her watch. 'Sister, it's nearly six o'clock. How about gathering up your suspicions and joining me for dinner?'

Mary Helen studied the young woman. Should she, or shouldn't she? She hesitated, but only for a minute.

* * *

'Hurry up, hon,' Jack called from the bedroom. Kate could hear the wire springs on the old bed creak.

'I'm still doing my face,' she called back, vacantly staring at herself in the bathroom mirror. Kate was never quite sure what she was doing to her face. But every night, faithfully, she smeared it with a creamy cleanser, dabbed it with astringent, and rubbed it with moisturizer.

'Your face looks fine to me,' he called back, 'and besides, that's not what I'm interested in. Come on!'

'What is it you are interested in?' Kate asked, massaging her neck in sweeping strokes, as the directions on her beauty preparations dictated.

'Right now, I can't decide whether I'm interested in wringing your neck for bringing that nun home for dinner or in just forgetting the whole thing and making mad, passionate love.'

Kate giggled. Gingerly, she crawled into her side of the big double bed. The old, brass monstrosity had been her parents'.

'And which interest seems to be winning out?' she asked, turning toward him. She propped herself up on one elbow and with the other hand began to slowly twist a strand of thick, red hair.

'You know damn well, but it won't get off the ground with you curling that piece of hair,' Jack said. 'What's on your mind, Kate?'

'Tonight, of course,' she said. 'Tell me, Jack, what did you think about Sister Mary Helen's suspicions?'

'I think if you stick with her, you'll crack the case,' Jack said. 'Now let's . . . '

'No, seriously,' Kate interrupted. 'Let me talk this out with you, please.'

'Murder at the dinner table is one thing, but bringing a murder to bed?'

'Please?'

Kate felt a warm glow as she watched Jack reach over and grab the cigarettes on the night stand. He offered her one and took one himself. I'm lucky to have him, she thought. What other man would put up with me? 'Shoot,' Jack said.

'What do you think?' she asked again.

'It's your case.' Jack inhaled. 'What's important is, what do you think?' Kate noted that he had switched to his Vice-Detail voice.

'I think her suspicions are well-founded. A thesis missing from the department chairman's office could be significant.'

'Are you sure it's missing?' Jack handed her an ashtray.

'We didn't come across one when we searched his office. I would have recognized the name Alves, as his secretary's. There is, moreover, the little matter of the slit in the coroner's seal. Maybe someone wanted it more than we did.'

'Go on.'

'Then, when the nuns called the people who had been interviewed, the older folks sounded nervous about the professor's influence on the young. Mary Helen suspects there are some things they don't want to say. Then, there is this Dom Sebastiao statue business.'

'What about it?' Jack asked, running his hand along her firm thigh.

Good God, the man was patient! 'I love you, Jack Bassetti,' Kate said. Leaning over, she kissed his forehead.

'If you love me, for God's sake, hurry up.' He groaned and turned over. 'Some women have headaches,' he said, running his free hand over her hip. 'You have murder cases. Hurry!'

'Dom Sebastiao — the legend or cult, if you want to call it that. Could the professor have thought he was Dom Sebastiao reincarnated? It sounds silly to us, but it could be real to someone who believes it. Our murders could be just the tip of the iceberg.'

'Speaking of icebergs.' Jack gentled her body closer to his. The wire springs creaked.

'One common denominator in this case is Professor Villanueva. The murdered girl, all the young people he helped came from the same part of Portugal.' Kate's eyes twinkled. 'And they all landed at the college.'

'Which proves?'

'Nothing.' Abruptly, Kate sat up. Jack groaned.

'How many kids did he sponsor?' he asked, running the tips of his fingers up her rigid spine.

Kate shivered with pleasure. 'Nine,' she said. 'Marina, Joanna, Tony — the gardener at the college — Luis, the janitor, and, of course, Leonel, who does the cooking. The two fellows no one seems to be able to reach on the phone, plus Mrs Rubiero's two nephews.'

Kate began to trace circles on the

comforter. 'Now Rubiero's nephews seem to have disappeared also. Lead or coincidence? Who knows?'

'You and Sister Mary Helen will find that out soon enough.' Jack lifted the bed covers, inviting her to slide down under. 'Aren't you two going to see Mrs Rubiero tomorrow?'

Kate nodded. 'Wait till Gallagher hears that!'

'That Mary Helen's quite a gal.' Jack pulled the sheet over his bare shoulder. 'She said she's been in the convent over fifty years. I've been thinking about that. That's some commitment. Do you think we could ever stick to anything for that long?'

Ignoring the question, Kate snuggled down in the soft bed close to his strong body. He felt warm. 'You know, Jack, it's the motive that really bothers me,' she said.

'Shit!' Jack exploded. Kate looked at him. Poor guy, she thought, drawing her slim finger up and down the back of his neck. She could feel him begin to relax.

Tenderly, he moved his broad hand under her granny gown. 'Damn these things,' he said, pushing the flannel aside. 'I don't know how grandpas managed to be so productive if grannies really wore all this.'

Kate giggled. 'Grannies,' she said, edging closer, 'were very cooperative.'

Seventh Day

'Fourteen forty-eight. This is it.' Sister Mary Helen pointed toward the third small bungalow from the corner. Kate pulled up in front and parked. The wooden-framed house, set back on two small, manicured patches of lawn, was painted a bright, clean white with dark green shutters. Several large pots of cadmium-red geraniums decorated the deep porch. The house had a well-cared-for look, as if somebody loved it.

Senhora Rubiero opened the front door before they rang the bell. 'Good morning, Sister.' She nodded deferentially toward Mary Helen. 'Please to come in.'

'Good morning, Senhora Rubiero.' Sister Mary Helen followed the short, rotund woman into the house. 'This is Officer Murphy from the San Francisco Police Department.' She motioned toward Kate, who flashed her badge. Mary Helen noticed a flash of fear in the woman's sharp, black eyes.

'So nice of you to let us come.' Kate smiled reassuringly. Senhora Rubiero relaxed a bit.

'Please, sit,' she said, waving to a mohair couch against one wall of the small living room. The room matched the outside of the house. Though freshly polished and well-cared-for, it smelled unused. It was probably what another generation would have referred to as the parlor and used strictly for important visitors. In this house, Mary Helen figured, most of the living probably goes on in a warm, cozy kitchen.

'What lovely handiwork.' Mary Helen fingered one of the delicate doilies covering the arms and back of the couch. 'Did you crochet these?' she asked.

'Yes, Sister.' The old woman blushed.

'Lovely.'

'Thank you.' Senhora Rubiero perched her squat body on the edge of an overstuffed chair across from Kate and Mary Helen.

There was an awkward moment of silence during which Mary Helen studied the woman. One glance told her that Senhora Rubiero was a no-nonsense person. Her black, laced shoes were definitely sensible and had been bought, no doubt, for comfort rather than style. A black jersey dress, properly pulled together in the front with a cameo pin, stretched across her shelflike bosom. The hem of the dress more than adequately covered the knees of her two sturdy legs. Besides the pin, her only touch of frivolity was a pair of earrings, if you could consider the small, gold balls frivolous.

Not a single gray hair escaped from the neatly rolled knot at the nape of her neck. They wouldn't dare, Mary Helen thought, observing the wide, strong hands that had rolled them there. A broad gold wedding band assured the old nun that Senhora Rubeiro was indeed a *senhora*.

This lady might blush, demur to nuns, and even be momentarily frightened of the police, but, underneath it all, she was one tough customer. Mary Helen liked her immediately. Eileen would have called it an instant feeling of kinship!

'Can I get you something to drink, to eat?' Senhora Rubiero spoke English haltingly, but very well. There would be no danger of misunderstanding. Whatever the woman had to say would be clearly understood. Mary Helen guessed she had probably come to this country as a young married woman.

'No, thank you, Senhora.' Kate answered for both of them. 'We are here on official business. We would like to ask you some questions about your two nephews.'

At the mention of the two young men, Senhora Rubiero's black eyes flashed anger. 'Carlos and Jose — two young fools. Ah, my poor sister — their mother . . . I promise her I take care. But, the young *stupidos* . . . '

190

Mary Helen watched, fascinated, as the woman's thick hands began to move as quickly and nimbly as her tongue. The subject of her nephews had completely taken away any inhibitions she might have had. She warmed to her subject.

'They come. They stay. They go. They say nothing. No hello. No goodbye. No *gracia, Tia*. How you call? Ingrates? And, ah my poor sister. What should I tell her?'

She paused to breathe and wring her hands. Mary Helen found it difficult to tell whether she was more upset about the ingratitude of her two nephews or about reporting their absence to her sister.

'If only my Alberto was here,' she said, tapping her wedding ring. 'He would take a care. They come home, eat, sleep, say nothing. But what is a poor woman to do? If only Alberto was here.' She blessed herself. Apparently, Alberto had gone to his eternal reward, one he had, no doubt, earned.

'I am only a woman,' she repeated, shaking her head sadly. Butler's couplet rang through Mary Helen's mind. 'Women, you know, do seldom fail, to make the stoutest man turn tail.' This had, no doubt, been the case with Alberto and the nephews.

'I cannot go to these hang-outs.' She spat out the last two words.

Kate perked up. 'Could you tell me about these hang-outs?' she asked, pulling a small notebook from her brown leather purse. 'Where are they located? Who do the boys go there with?'

Senhora Rubiero's eyes narrowed. 'I don't know where they go. They never tell me, the *tia*. They go with other young fools . . . other *solteiros*.' Realizing that her two visitors did not understand her last word, Senhora Rubiero translated. '*Solteiros*. How you call? Bachelors — bachelors who never want to marry.'

Kate nodded. 'Who were these others?' she asked, her pencil poised.

Senhora Rubiero ignored Kate's question. She didn't even seem to notice the poised pencil. Jockeying her ample hips into a more comfortable position, she continued. 'When we come from the old country, we work hard, pay back our benefactors. Help our relatives back home.' Mary Helen recognized the familiar ring. A generation gap in any nationality sounds the same.

'Not like now. Now they think money comes with the sun. Fool around. Don't care for family. Live together, boy and girl, without marry.'

Mary Helen could feel Kate stiffen at the 'live together without marry' line. Direct hit,

Mary Helen thought, remembering her dinner last night. The old woman paused dramatically. Obviously, she had given this lecture many times before. Most recently, probably, to her nephews.

'The Sister, she understand.' Senhora Rubiero wagged her head.

'Have you any idea who these friends are, Senhora?' Kate asked.

'Other young fools.' Senhora Rubiero's eyes darted toward the phone. 'I hear them talking. Luis, Tony, my friend Erma's cousin Manuel, Leonel, Jose. He now calls himself Joe. Fernando, Salvador, Fatima's boy, Angelo, some more I don't know. They speak of Sebastiao. He will come, a savior. Save them, save Portugal. *Madre de Deus.*' She blessed herself. 'Save them! *Stupidos!* Only work. Work to be saved. Hard work will save them. No savior.'

Sebastiao. There it was again. 'Who did they think this Sebastiao would be?' Mary Helen asked.

The old woman shrugged, 'Crazy, *si?*'

'Luis, Tony, Manuel, Leonel, Jose, who calls himself Joe, Fernando, Salvador, and Angelo,' Kate read back from her note pad. 'Do you have last names or phone numbers for any of these fellows?'

Senhora Rubiero pushed herself out of the

193

overstuffed chair and waddled toward a back room.

'What do you make of it?' Mary Helen asked Kate as soon as the old woman had gone.

'If the last names jibe, these are the same people the professor helped, and at least four of them are at the college.' She shot a quick glance at Mary Helen. 'Maybe we've hit upon the link. Maybe it's this Sebastiao business.'

'For the men, perhaps — but Marina and Joanna? And why would someone murder Joanna?'

'Maybe both men and women belong to this — what should I call it? — cult. Or maybe Joanna was on to something. Maybe something rotten. Maybe that's why Senhora Rubiero's nephews have vanished, pronto. Afraid Joanna would have blown the whistle. And maybe one of them decided to make sure she wouldn't.'

Mary Helen suppressed a grin. It amused her to hear this trim, well-dressed, cultured young lady talk like a cop.

'What I can't figure is, if they were into something, something they all wanted, why kill the professor? Why destroy the goose that lays the golden egg?'

Mary Helen resisted the temptation to tell her that only a *professora* could lay eggs.

'Perhaps the professor wasn't all he was cracked up to be,' she said, remembering Leonel's outburst. Calling your savior a devil, a filthy animal, a flesh-eater, and a bloodsucker could hardly be construed as complimentary.

She was just about to relate the incident to Kate when Senhora Rubiero reappeared in the doorway. She was carrying a small, flowered address book, well-worn at the edges, which she handed to Kate.

'By the way, Senhora,' Kate asked, 'did you ever hear your nephew talking to any women? Marina or Joanna, perhaps?'

'If they talked with girls, I would not be so worried. Maybe marry, settle down.' The older woman shook her head sadly. 'Now, some tea? Coffee?'

'No, thank you.' Kate rose from the couch. 'We're on duty, and I'd like to question some of these young men you have mentioned.' Senhora Rubiero looked disappointed to be losing her audience.

'May I keep this for a few days?' Kate held up the address book.'

'Si, Officer.' The senhora bowed graciously and escorted her guests to the front door. 'What numbers I need, I know.' She smiled broadly, every one of her strong, white teeth as straight as a die. Mary Helen ran her tongue across her own slightly overlapping front teeth. And I bet every single tooth in her mouth is hers, she thought, smiling back.

★ ★ ★

'That's some old lady!' Kate flipped on the ignition in the Plymouth. 'I was beginning to wonder if those two nephews might have disappeared out of self-defense.'

'Could be.' Grinning, Sister Mary Helen fastened her seat belt. 'But that would not account for what happened to the others. Or for the reason Leonel is so concerned about their leaving — how did he put it? — 'poof, without even a goodbye.''

Kate faced her passenger. 'Leonel worried about the others leaving? Poof? You never mentioned that before!'

'I must have,' Mary Helen said quickly. She wouldn't want Kate to think for one moment that she was withholding evidence. Why, she was just beginning to feel that they had struck up a bit of a partnership, and she, for one, was enjoying every minute of it. Not the murder part, of course, but the detecting. She didn't want to be dropped. The old nun could feel her face redden. For a moment she felt ridiculous. But hadn't someone once said, 'If we err in our liking of detective stories, we err with Plato'? Well, if they hadn't, they surely should have!

'I'm sure I told you.' She added a little emphasis. 'Just before you picked up Leonel, he told me he was worried about some in the group the professor had brought to this country.' She glanced over at Kate. The young woman's jaw was firm.

'Go on,' Kate said.

'Well, that's all he said. Four of them were missing. Poof! And he was worried about Joanna.'

'Which four?'

'A Carlos and Jose. Those must be Mrs Rubiero's nephews. And two Manuels.'

'Is that everything you know?'

'Everything I can think of,' Mary Helen answered meekly, trying to erase the slit in the coroner's seal from her mind. There was really no use getting into that.

After a few moments of silence, Kate pointed to her notebook and to Senhora Rubiero's worn address book on the seat between them. 'There must be hundreds of Tonys and Luises and Manuels in the Portuguese community,' she said. 'First thing we'd better do is find out if we are talking about the same people. Check the book against the list in my notebook, will you please, Sister?' Relieved, Mary Helen picked up the two books. They were still partners.

They had just merged on to 280 heading toward the city when Mary Helen finished her checking. 'The last names and phone numbers are the same. We are talking about the same people.' She didn't know whether to feel happy or sad. On the one hand, she was glad that everything seemed to be narrowing down to a few young people Professor Villanueva had sponsored. She imagined that would make discovering the killer easier. On the other hand, she was sad that all the evidence was beginning to point to the murderer as being one of them, someone the sisters all knew. It seemed now she had been right about that from the beginning. The murderer was not some poor, demented psychotic who had wandered on to the hill, but someone who had been, or still was, at the college.

The two rode for several miles in a comfortable silence, each lost in her own thoughts. There wasn't much traffic on a Saturday morning. A soft autumn sun on the Peninsula hit against the low, rolling hills to their left. It made little sparks of light bounce across the deep, black-blue water of Crystal Springs Lake. A small, green boat cut gently through the water — probably a Water Department caretaker making sure the lake was safe to supply the City with drinking water. The scene was so peaceful, so pastoral, Mary Helen forgot for a moment the horrors of the past few days.

'Look ahead.' Kate's voice jarred her back into reality. She was pointing toward the city. 'Fog!'

Sure enough. Ahead of them, San Francisco was wrapped in a cocoon of gray fog.

'I guess we had better head straight into that mess and up to the college to question Tony and Luis again.' Kate changed to the fast lane on the freeway. 'Do you think they'll be at work today?'

'I don't see why not,' Mary Helen answered, remembering that she, too, wanted to talk to Tony.

'This time I think I'll ask them about their connection with Dom Sebastiao. Maybe that's the angle.'

'Maybe.' Mary Helen was distracted. Something about that Sebastiao bothered her. What was it? Something she had wanted to tell Kate.

'I think I'd better question Leonel again, too.' Kate glanced over at Mary Helen.

Leonel! That was it! Poor, volatile Leonel and his outbursts against the professor. That is what she had wanted to tell Kate when Senhora Rubiero had reappeared in the living

199

room. Maybe 'wanted to' was a bit too strong. Perhaps 'felt she should' would be a more honest evaluation.

Quickly, Mary Helen related the incidents, carefully omitting to tell where she had run into Leonel. 'And so you see, Kate,' she concluded, trying her best not to use her schoolmarm voice, 'although I'm not sure why, some one of those fellows could have been so disillusioned with the professor that he ended up hating him enough to bludgeon him to death with his own statue.' Mary Helen gave a triumphant smile. But as soon as her last word echoed in her ears, she realized what she'd said. She hoped Kate hadn't. She had.

'Like Leonel?' Kate's mouth formed a hard, straight line.

'Like any one of them,' Mary Helen shot back, feeling a little as she felt when she miscounted the trump. 'Leonel was the only one I heard express it.' She tried to recover.

'Why didn't you tell me this before?'

'It didn't seem significant.'

'You were afraid it would implicate Leonel, weren't you?'

No, the old nun thought, not implicate, vindicate. Sister Mary Helen waited several minutes before she thought it might be safe to speak. Long enough, she calculated, for two

200

Irish tempers to cool down. She hoped she reckoned the cooling-down period correctly, because she liked Kate Murphy. 'What I can't figure out is Joanna's connection,' she offered mildly.

'That's a tough one,' Kate answered, quietly. 'I know there must be some connection between the two crimes. We're looking for a direct connection, something that will link the murderer with both Joanna and the professor. Now also with the Sebastiao business. Maybe we're missing the real connection. Some indirect link we haven't even noticed yet.'

Carefully, Kate veered the Plymouth over into the slow lane. She turned off the freeway at the first Daly City exit. 'I'll stop and give Denny a call,' she said, pulling into a gas station on her right. 'I'll ask him to meet me at the college in twenty minutes.' Kate checked her watch. 'He can help me question these fellows again.' She rummaged through her purse for some change.

Sitting in the car, Mary Helen watched Kate in the phone booth. She had removed one earring and was talking rapidly. Probably explaining the whole interview with Senhora Rubiero to Inspector Gallagher. Mary Helen could just see him sitting back, loosening his tie, saying nothing, rolling his stubby cigar around in his mouth. Poor fellow probably couldn't have shoved a word in sideways, even if he wanted to.

Small wisps of fog escaping from San Francisco blew into Daly City and whipped around the phone booth and parked car. Mary Helen felt the chill. She pulled her jacket tightly around her.

She stared at the large oil stain by the gas pump. It was slick and black against the gray cement. Small, round bubbles of water from the wet fog stood out on the surface. Hostile properties, she mused, staring at the oil resisting the moisture. The substances just don't mix. Like the two murders — Professor Villanueva's and Joanna's. Her instincts told her something was off kilter. But what? The connection wasn't right. What had Kate said? 'Maybe the connection is indirect.' Could there be two separate connections, two separate motives, like these two separate substances on the damp cement of the gas station — two that do not mix?

Or perhaps . . . A thought shot through her mind like an electric shock. It left her dazed and clammy cold. She hated to allow it in a second time, but she had to. Any detective worthy of her salt had to look at all the possibilities. Could it be possible that there were two different murderers? She swallowed hard.

'What's the matter with you?' Kate jumped into the car and slammed the door. 'You're as white as a ghost. Are you okay?'

'I just had a horrible thought.' Mary Helen could hear the desolate ring in her own voice. How she hoped Kate would say she was wrong.

'What is it?' Kate asked.

'You said that maybe we were missing the connection between the two murders because it was an indirect one . . . one we never thought of . . . like two motives for murder. Well, one thing we have never really thought of at all is the possibility of two murderers!'

Kate said nothing. She started the car and zig-zagged her way through the traffic toward Mount St Francis College for Women.

Mary Helen stared out the car window. Immediately, she began to reason with God. Dear Lord, think of poor Therese. She's on the seventh day of her novena, the one she began to catch one murderer of one victim. Now look what You are letting happen! Two murders, and now maybe two murderers! How, in heaven's name, can You do that to poor, high-strung Therese!

Mary Helen was glad God seldom talked back, because she was pretty sure she knew what He would say. 'Hold on! People murdering one another is not exactly the way I plan things! But relax, old dear, and stick with Me. We'll work it out!' And she knew He was oh, so right.

* * *

Inspector Gallagher was waiting for them when they arrived at the college. Mary Helen spotted him immediately. His bald head stood out like a shiny buoy in the sea of slender, jeans-clad Saturday students gushing from the main entrance.

The Angelus bell began to toll twelve noon. Its low rhythmic notes rang out from the college bell tower and reverberated through the dripping fog.

Gallagher was all business after nodding to Mary Helen. 'I've located two of the boys. Luis is supposed to be working on the second floor, main building. Leonel in the kitchen. They tell me Tony is somewhere on the grounds. We can look him up later. You want to requestion these guys — using the cult angle?'

'Right!' Slamming the car door behind her, Kate followed Gallagher up the stairs of the entrance to the main college building.

Probably going to talk to Luis first, Mary

Helen concluded, feeling a bit left out. She was tempted to ask if she could go along when her stomach rumbled. She decided to follow its lead. Skirting the main building, she ducked into the sisters' dining room where Eileen and Anne waited, as eager to hear about her visit to Senhora Rubiero as she was to tell.

* * *

The two inspectors found Luis guiding a heavy floor polisher back and forth across the already highly polished second-floor hall. The machine formed a glossy wave across the parquet as the young man maneuvered it from side to side. His movements were punctuated with a dull thud against either baseboard. Luis stopped abruptly when he saw them, his hand still clutching the vibrating polisher. The color drained from his sallow face.

'We'd like to ask you a few more questions,' Kate called over the hum of the polisher.

Turning off the machine, Luis limped toward them. He was a small, slight man with wide, frightened eyes.

'Okay.' He shoved his hands into his overall pockets. He looked to Kate like someone who was used to being bullied.

'Is there some place we can talk?' Gallagher asked.

Nodding, Luis led the way down the hall. After fumbling with a heavy set of keys, he let them into a narrow storage room.

'I know no more about murder. I told-a you everything I know,' he began as soon as they entered the room. The color had begun to return to his face.

'I'm sure you did.' Kate perched herself on the edge of a nicked table. 'What we want to ask you about is something else. What do you know about Dom Sebastiao?'

The young man blanched. Kate could almost smell fear. '*Nada*,' he said, too quickly.

'Nothing? Are you sure?' Gallagher moved in closer.

'Only a little.' Luis shifted uncomfortably. Obviously, he was not used to lying.

'Tell us,' Kate urged. 'It would help us find this murderer.'

'Only I know that the professor, he talks of it. Helps us to come to this country. To marry. To make the money. Some day, he say, we will return to Portugal rich men.'

He looked so hopeful that Kate was sure he had forgotten for the moment that the professor and his promises were dead.

'Where did you meet the professor?' she asked.

'I read about in the newspaper at home. He offers to bring young people over.'

'For free?'

Luis stared at her with disbelief. 'Polica-lady,' he said, shaking his head sadly, 'nothing is for free.'

'How much did you pay him?' Gallagher asked.

Luis calculated silently for a few moments. 'Ten thousand dollars, your money.'

'And he brought over nine young people from your area?'

Luis nodded. Kate didn't need to calculate ninety thousand dollars. Behind her, she heard Gallagher curse softly. She knew without even looking at him that he was enraged.

'Not bad for social work, if you can get it,' she heard him mutter.

'Were Carlos and Jose Gomes among the nine?' Kate asked.

Luis nodded.

'Their aunt is very worried about them. They both seem to have vanished. Do you have any idea where they may have gone?'

Luis shook his head. Kate thought she saw fear in his eyes.

'Senhora Rubiero told us that the Gomes boys talked to you often on the phone. Are you sure you don't have any idea what happened to them?'

'No.' Small white saliva bubbles began to form at the corner of Luis's mouth. Nervously, he checked the luminous dial on his watch. 'The floor. I gotta finish. They no like if I take too long. Okay I go?'

'Okay.' Kate watched the slender young man dart from the storage room.

'He knows something he's afraid to tell,' Gallagher said as he and Kate cut a crooked path through the small groups of students bunched on the staircase. 'He's not our murderer, though.'

'What makes you say that?' Kate followed him out of the building and down the side path toward the kitchen and Leonel.

'Too scared to kill. Did you see that guy, Kate? Everything about him looks like a frightened animal.'

'Yeah, but let's not forget, Denny, what frightened animals do when they are backed into a corner.'

Gallagher shrugged, but said nothing. Kate knew he was right.

★ ★ ★

Leonel was easy to spot. His tightly curled head stuck out among the stainless steel pots. He stared belligerently at the two inspectors walking across the kitchen toward him.

Kate's eyes met his. 'Leonel, we'd like to ask you some questions.'

'What more you want with me?' He wiped his damp hands on his butcher apron and squared his shoulders. 'I told you everything I know in your jail!'

'Everything you knew about the professor's murder. But we'd like to ask you about something else. What do you know about this Dom Sebastiao business?'

Leonel's hollow, mocking laugh rocked through the kitchen. Startled, several members of the kitchen crew turned to stare.

'Come.' Leonel motioned to the two officers and led them out the back door to the kitchen stoop.

'Tell us what you know about it, son.' Gallagher stuck a match against the stone wall and relit his cigar. The small puff of smoke blended into the fog.

'I know that it is good — how you say? fitting? — that the professor was killed with the statue. An act of God!' His voice was venomous.

'Why do you say that?' Kate prodded him.

'Because he tricks us . . . makes fools of us . . . At home we are poor. He lends us money to come here. Now, we must pay back and pay back.'

He slammed a clenched fist against the door jamb. 'We think at first he is like Dom Sebastiao. A savior . . . for the good of all. He will save Portugal . . . make it a powerful country once more. We will become rich here. Go home . . . marry. Become famous in our country. But no. He fools us, and we are the fools. He does not keep his promises. He controls our lives . . . keeps us poor. And then Carlos, Manuel, Jose . . . they disappear . . . Where are they? When I ask where, he shrugs.' His muscular body trembled with rage. 'Bloodsucker! Whoever killed him was a *santo*!' Closing his eyes, he leaned back against the kitchen door. Small beads of perspiration stood out on his ashen face.

'Did you kill him?' Kate asked in a firm, quiet voice.

'No.'

'Do you know who did?'

Leonel did not answer. Kate studied the young man. 'I asked if you know who did?' For a moment, she thought she caught a shadow of terror in his dark eyes. Then slowly, deliberately, he shook his head.

Without hesitating, Kate switched her questions. 'What about Joanna?' she pressed. 'Why would anybody want to kill her?'

Leonel's head snapped back as if he had been slapped. Involuntary tears welled up in his eyes. 'I cannot know,' he said, wiping his eyes with the back of his broad hand. 'Jesus, I cannot know. Unless she finds out too much.'

Desolate was the only word Kate could think of as she watched Leonel shake his head in bewilderment. We've hit a dead end, she thought, looking toward Gallagher. The older man simply shrugged.

Kate touched Leonel's shoulder. 'Thank you,' she said gently. 'Be sure to get in touch with us if you think of anything that might help.'

As the two police officers walked away, the tall young man crumpled on to the stoop. Burying his face in his butcher apron, he wept.

Kate glanced sideways at her partner. Gallagher was straightening his tie and looking uncomfortable.

'Where are we, Denny?' she asked, more to distract him than anything else.

'We better be getting somewhere soon,' he said. 'The Chief called this morning while you were down the Peninsula. Must be feeling the heat from the Mayor's office.'

'Think we're getting close?' Kate hoped Gallagher hadn't noticed the sudden eagerness in her voice. Not very professional, but what a plum for the 'odd couple' to wind up the Holy Hill murders in less than two weeks!

How she'd relish rubbing that into the guys at Detail.

Gallagher cleared his throat. 'Let's see. That Leonel is strong enough and mad enough to have killed the guy. But you know as well as I do, we haven't got enough evidence to charge him.'

'We have his prints on that statue,' Kate said. 'But he claims he was just putting it back for Marina. Could be.'

'And Joanna? Would he have killed Joanna?'

'I don't think he did it.' Kate buttoned her wool plaid jacket against the biting wind.

'Well, then, where are we, Denny?' Kate repeated. 'Think we're at least making progress?'

'Well, we've pretty well eliminated Luis, right?'

'Right.'

'And Leonel?'

'Unless we can place him definitely at the scene.'

'That's progress.'

'Progress?' Kate stared at her partner, disappointed. 'All we've done is eliminate one suspect and raise a few unanswered questions about a second. Who have we left?'

'Mrs Rubiero's whole address book.'

Kate groaned. Even Superwoman couldn't get through that whole address book by the end of the week.

'Cheer up, Katie girl.' Gallagher patted her on the back. 'We're ahead of where we were an hour ago. At least, we know of two who probably didn't do it.'

Suddenly, Kate felt tired and hungry. 'Want to walk to the coffee shop down the hill before we go looking for the gardener?' she asked.

Nodding his head, Gallagher shoved his hands deep into the pockets of his trousers and followed.

★ ★ ★

By the time Mary Helen, Eileen, and Anne left the dining room, the persistent autumn sun had started to burn off the fog. A crisp wind whipped around the side of the main college building, chilling the three nuns who stood on the lawn, still talking.

'What do you think about there being two murderers?' Mary Helen asked, eager to pick her friends' brains.

'Isn't one enough?' Anne asked.

'One too many, if you ask me,' Eileen said. 'But Mary Helen may well be correct . . . two murderers with two distinct motives. Double trouble!'

'What about one murderer? Joanna saw him, and then he had to murder her, too?

213

That's a good motive.' Obviously, Anne was reluctant to admit to two murderers.

'Yes, dear — except Joanna could not have seen the murderer. We all know that!' Eileen jointed out.

'How do we all know that?' Anne imitated Eileen's slight brogue.

'Because Marina told you so, Anne dear. Joanna had gone out of town that night. She called her from San Jose.'

'But we really don't know for sure, do we? How does Marina know she really was in San Jose when she called? She disappeared right after that. She may have lied to Marina and come back to the college. Really, no one knows exactly where she was. Except her murderer.'

Anne's declaration was met with silence. 'Besides,' she added sheepishly, her real point becoming clear, 'if you think there are two murderers, please keep it to yourselves. Therese is driving everyone absolutely bananas whining about being killed in our very own cloister. If she thinks she has to watch out for two fiends, instead of one, there'll be no enduring her.'

Mary Helen couldn't swallow her guffaw fast enough. Murder was no laughing matter, but human nature surely was. Her laugh burst across the silent campus. Several young women swung around at the unexpected noise.

'Oh, oh, both my appointments spotted me,' Anne checked her watch. 'I've about two minutes to get to my office. Girl's pregnant, I think. One says she wants to be a nun.'

'Different girls, I hope!' Mary Helen said lightly, secretly grateful once again that she was in history and not campus ministry.

Smiling, Anne tried to roll her eyes like Therese's. Then, briskly, she walked toward her basement office.

Eileen stomped her feet to keep warm. 'I'd better go, too.' She frowned toward the windows of the Hanna Memorial. 'However, if luck is on my side, they may have given my job away. I'll see you later, old dear.'

★ ★ ★

Mary Helen watched her friend go, her own mind spinning. Murderers and policemen, hidden motives, unknown connections whirled around. Altogether, it was very unsettling! What she needed was some — what did Anne call it? — 'space.' That was it. She needed space. But where? 'In green old gardens hidden away, from sight of revel and sound of strife. Here may I live what life I please . . . ' For the life of her, she couldn't remember the rest of the verse, but the message was clear. Her 'spot' would be ideal.

Swooping into her bedroom, she grabbed her brand new mystery novel. Deftly, she wrapped it in her plastic prayer book cover. She placed the ribbon marker on page one. A sweater. If she was going to enjoy an afternoon in her spot, she'd need a sweater. That cold stone bench seeped right through polyester. Her big, bulky Aran knit would be perfect.

Slamming the convent door behind her, Mary Helen shook it hard to make sure it was locked. With poor Therese so twittery, there was no sense leaving the door ajar.

Trudging up the hill from the Sisters' Residence, she suddenly realized how tired she was. Her legs had no push. Her neck and shoulders ached. If she didn't know better, she would have sworn that someone had siphoned her pep. An old Model T without gas, she thought, taking the small, winding path leading to her stone bench. And no wonder she was dragging. These last seven days had been hectic. She was very wise to take the afternoon off to act retired. Just sit and relax and read a good, clean, objective murder mystery, one in which you didn't know the victim personally and in which the killer was easy to guess.

She breathed deeply. The wild, woodsy smell of the hillside cleared her head. 'To linger silent among the healthful woods, musing on such things as are worthy of a wise and good man.' In this case, woman. That Horace surely knew what he was talking about. She inhaled again. Dry pine needles crunched under her walking shoes. Carefully, she skirted a small, broken limb that had fallen from the dollar eucalyptus.

The sight of eucalyptus, Scotch pine, and untamed juniper flourishing right beside a busy campus in the middle of a busy city lifted her spirits. This lovely foliage grew — oblivious of any of the human beings around it, untouched by human frailty, unharmed by human hatred or greed or jealousy or even murder.

It was then she spotted Tony coming down the path toward her. He was wearing mud-spattered work clothes and dragging a rusty shovel. A small cloud of dust followed him. He was on her list. She should talk to him. Find out what he knew. But this afternoon she just didn't feel like it. She wanted to be alone on her hillside, thinking her own thoughts. She didn't want to talk about murder or motives or alibis. She didn't even want to be polite. Fortunately, she didn't have to be.

'What are you doing here, Sister?' Tony asked, rather gruffly, she thought.

None of your business! was the first retort that popped into her mind. 'Going to the clearing,' she said mildly, pointing toward it with her plastic-covered book.

'Oh,' he said, apparently not knowing what to say next. Mary Helen thought she smelled alcohol on his breath. They stood, looking at each other, waiting for the other to make the first move.

His eyes were glazed. For a moment Mary Helen said nothing, just met his stare with a well-practiced, schoolmarm stare of her own.

Tony took a step toward her. Then she was sure she smelled it; the acrid and unmistakable odor of stale wine.

Gripping the handle of his shovel, he steadied himself. Mary Helen was annoyed. All she needed to complete her day was an obnoxious drunk!

'If you'll excuse me now,' Mary Helen said, primly edging to Tony's left. With one unsteady step he blocked her way, beginning to raise his shovel.

'Is there something you wish to discuss?' She struggled to keep the quaver out of her voice.

Suddenly, from several yards below, Kate Murphy's voice called, 'Tony! Is that you?'

Mary Helen listened to the slap of four footsteps coming toward them. There went her knees again. This time they felt like spaghetti. Kate and Inspector Gallagher rounded the corner. Thank goodness.

Tony dropped the shovel. 'Yeah. Who wants to know?' He took two or three staggering steps toward them.

'Police,' Gallagher barked, jerking his badge from his back pocket.

'Look who's here,' Kate smiled when she saw Mary Helen. 'I hope you're not doing our work for us.'

Sister Mary Helen's hand shook as she grabbed Kate's arm and pulled her to the side. 'Thank God, you're here,' she whispered, trying to keep her voice from quaking. 'That young man is very intoxicated and very angry. You don't suppose he could be our murderer, do you? There's something in his eyes . . .'

Kate looked amused. 'Negative,' she whispered back, cutting into the middle of Mary Helen's sentence. 'Remember — I told you he had an alibi for the night the professor was killed. I checked. He was in a bar in Santa Clara with dozens of other Portuguese who'll swear to it, not to mention the bartender. In the trade, we call that airtight!'

'Airtight? Are you sure?'

Kate nodded. 'Sorry, Sister.'

Mary Helen frowned over at Tony. Unless there were two murderers, she thought.

Gallagher fired questions which the young man answered in monosyllables.

Kate returned to her first question. 'What are you up to?'

Mary Helen took a long deep breath. If I had any sense at all, I'd go straight to my room and lock the door and lie down, she thought. But I'll be switched if I'll let one ugly scene with one ugly man intimidate me!

'I'm going to that favorite spot of mine to sit for a while,' she said, indicating her book.

'Pray for us while you're there.' Kate patted her arm. Mary Helen didn't have the energy to explain about her plastic cover. Later.

'And, Sister, by the way. How about dinner tonight? Jack enjoyed you so much. Besides, I'd like to talk to you about the two-murderer theory. We'll have something simple. Maybe pick up Chinese.' Kate seemed genuinely eager.

'I'd love that,' Mary Helen said.

'Good. We'll question this guy. Go downtown to do the paper work and then I'll pick you up. Around six.'

Mary Helen settled comfortably on the cold stone bench. It took several minutes for her breathing and heartbeat to return to normal and a little longer for her knees to lose that shaky feeling.

Closing her eyes, she bundled her Aran knit sweater around her and pulled the thick collar over her ears. The sun was warm on her legs. When she started up the path, she'd been tired; after her little encounter, she was exhausted. She needed a nap. Not here, not now. She should think. Put this whole thing together. Yet her entire body felt drugged; her energy sapped; her limbs weary. She fought to stay awake. Suddenly, she felt all of seventy, or was it seventy . . . Within minutes, the old nun had fallen into a sound sleep.

★ ★ ★

'Our friend Tony was really into his cups.' Inspector Gallagher followed Kate down the campus driveway into the parking lot.

'It didn't seem to loosen his tongue nor improve his disposition.' Kate leaned against the fender of the Plymouth. 'What do you make of this afternoon, Denny?'

'That little guy. Luis. He may be innocent, but he knows something. And he's scared shitless to tell it. I'd wager it has something to do with the professor and this Sebastiao business. Agreed?'

'Agreed.' Kate said. 'And he may be our

221

best bet. Not used to lying. Did you notice?'

'Yep.' Gallagher fumbled in his jacket pocket for a brand new cigar.

'Wish we could locate those two nephews of Senhora Rubiero's. And the two missing Manuels — Noia and Sousa. They might be able to tell us something that would wind this case up.' Kate did not relish going through the entire Rubiero address book.

Watching a small group of chattering students cross the asphalt, Kate felt a momentary twinge of envy as they laughed, piled into a tiny Volkswagen, and squealed out of the parking lot. Saturday night, and they could have cared less about murders and murderers and solving cases.

'Do you think there may be something to this two-murderer theory?' she asked, watching the Volkswagen taillights disappear down the driveway.

'Now you want two murderers?'

'Just a feeling.'

'Don't give me that women's intuition crap.' Gallagher rummaged through his pants pockets for a match.

Kate chose not to take up the gauntlet. 'We can't seem to find one suspect who could have committed both crimes,' she said evenly.

Gallagher grunted. 'Maybe we haven't found the right suspect,' he said. 'Or maybe you're right, and this two-killer theory is the way to go. One guy could have killed the professor, and a second guy could have killed the girl.'

'Why *guy*?'

'I don't know.' Gallagher shrugged. 'I guess a strong gal could have hit that hard. But the only woman even near either scene was that cute little secretary, Marina, with the innocent eyes. She hardly seems the type.'

'Don't give me that chauvinistic crap.' Tit for tat, Kate thought. 'What is the type?' she asked, watching Gallagher get his cigar and match together. She was always relieved when he finally made contact.

'Now that clown, Tony. He's the type. An obnoxious bastard. But we already know he has an airtight alibi for one of the nights in question. I can see why the bartender remembers him.'

'But maybe not for the day Joanna was killed.'

'Right. We'll get on that Monday, too.'

'I think Sister Mary Helen was genuinely frightened of Tony. Said there was something in his eyes. Maybe she had a point.'

'For crissake, Kate, she said Leonel had nice eyes and, therefore, couldn't be a killer. Now there's something wrong with this guy's eyes that says he can be. You've just run across a real eye nut! And eyes are not admissible evidence in a murder case.'

Kate couldn't resist. 'But they are the windows of the soul,' she said. Opening her car door, she threw her purse on the seat beside her. 'See you downtown, Denny. Want to split the paperwork?'

'Okay,' he said, moving toward his Ford.

The two car doors slammed simultaneously. Officers Murphy and Gallagher merged slowly on to Turk Street and headed downtown to the Hall of Justice.

★ ★ ★

After coffee, Kate drove Sister Mary Helen home. The poor old nun had looked exhausted during dinner, she seemed delighted when Kate suggested they all turn in early. The ride from 34th Avenue to the college was a quiet one, punctuated mostly by yawns. As soon as Kate saw Mary Helen safely inside the convent, she hurried back to Jack.

The moment she opened the front door, she knew he was angry. The loud thud of pots banging against the kitchen drainboard reverberated into the small entrance hall. A cupboard door crashed shut.

'Hi, hon. I'm back,' she called, hanging her coat in the hall closet. Cautiously, she peeked into the kitchen. All evening she'd had the uneasy feeling that Jack was building up to something, but she couldn't quite put her finger on what.

Jack, shirt sleeves rolled to his elbow, stood at the sink wiping silverware and slamming it into the drawer.

'I got Sister home okay.' She tiptoed across the room and planted a light kiss on his cheek. 'Thanks so much for cleaning up, pal . . . ' She was about to add, 'I love you,' when Jack flung the towel on the kitchen table.

'That's it!' Removing his chef's apron, he threw it in a heap with the towel.

Kate had never seen Jack quite like this before. He was furious. She really didn't know what to do. The wrath of the patient man . . . what was the proverb? Beware the wrath of the patient man. Up to this point, Jack Bassetti had been a very patient man. 'What is it?' she asked meekly.

'I have had it with this living together business. I don't know what the hell is wrong with us! It's the woman who is supposed to feel used and violated. The man is supposed to be able to change his shirt and whistle on his way. Our whole relationship is backassed!' He slammed an open palm on the kitchen table for emphasis.

'Damn it, Kate.' He was shouting now, his Italian in crescendo. 'At the risk of sounding like the heroine in a B movie — either marry me, or I'm leaving!'

Suddenly, Kate felt as if she had been punched in the stomach. She knew by the determined set of his lips that even when his temper cooled, he meant it. So this was it the showdown.

'Well, say something!'

She opened her mouth to speak, but couldn't. An ache closed her throat. Jack stood before her, stiff with anger, waiting for her answer.

'Well?' he repeated.

Quick tears flooded her eyes. Kate never cried. She hated to cry, yet the tears ran unchecked down her cheeks. She fumbled for a Kleenex. She tried to speak again, but couldn't. 'I love you,' she managed finally.

Jack thawed a little. 'Here, sit down.' He pulled out one of the kitchen chairs. 'I'll pour a couple of glasses of brandy. Let's talk.'

A little of the anger had left his voice. Kate was glad. Sniffling, she slipped her hand into his. He squeezed it. 'I really do love you,' she said.

'I love you, too, Kate. But I mean it!'

Kate rolled the rich, brown liquor around in the snifter, trying to think. 'Can we talk about it after this homicide at the college is solved? You know, Jack, it's really on my mind. I can hardly think of anything else.' She sniffed.

'That's an excuse, Kate. If it isn't this case, it will be another. You've got to decide.' Jack was coldly logical.

Kate stared into her glass. She had always dreaded this moment. She had hoped it would never come. Yet she knew it was inevitable. She knew Jack wanted to settle down, raise a family. But could she? 'I'll never give an inch to any man,' she had told Ma years ago. Then, she had meant it, too. The police shrink would probably have a field day figuring out her childhood traumas, her built-in views of masculine and feminine roles, and all the rest. All she knew was that up to now she had needed to feel independent, to be successful in a man's world, never to give an inch. But tonight she wasn't quite sure.

'Marriage is such a big step,' she said finally.

'I know. But we've had more than enough time to test it out. I think what it gets down to, Kate, is this. Do you really love me?' Jack set his glass down.

'Of course I love you.'

'Enough to make a commitment?'

'I've made one, or I wouldn't still be here.'

'I mean a permanent, legal, sacramental one. Do you remember what Sister Mary Helen said tonight about her fifty-year commitment?'

Kate remembered. She had hoped bringing Sister Mary Helen home would somehow put jack's mind at ease about their relationship. Instead, the whole damn thing had backfired. The old nun had just bitten into an egg roll when Jack brought it up. 'Every commitment, mine or anybody else's is a risk,' she had answered, 'because you must make choices, give up some things in order to have others. But, if you are sure of your feelings you are willing, in fact, eager, to take the risk, really love someone. And in my case,' she added matter-of-factly, 'I've never stopped being glad I risked it! Please pass the almond chicken.'

'My question still stands.' Jack's voice broke into Kate's thoughts. 'Do you love me enough to marry me, or do I move out tomorrow?'

'You don't mean it?'

'I do.'

'Is that a threat?' Kate's eyes leveled for the challenge. Even as she spoke the words, she realized it was a helluva time to save face.

Jack shook his head in exasperation. 'You have got to be the most goddam, stubborn Irishman . . . Irishwoman that God ever created, and I must be nuts to want you.'

Jack grabbed her clenched fists. 'Kate,' he said, 'it is not a threat. It is more like a goddam plea. Will you please marry me?'

Everything in her heart wanted to shout, 'Yes, I love you. I'll marry you. A sudden tingle of yearning rushed through her whole body. She loved him. She loved that kind, funny, wild Eye-talian just as much as he loved her. And love was a fling of the heart, not a matter for the head.

'Kate,' Jack repeated, 'will you marry me?'

Standing, she slipped her hands into his and pulled him up. Without a word, she led him through the kitchen, turning off the lights. Bewildered, Jack followed. She stopped. In the darkened kitchen, she pressed her body against his, put her arms tightly around his waist, and rested her head against his chest.

'What the hell are you doing?' Jack asked, his arms enveloping her.

'Ask me to marry you again,' she whispered.

'In the dark? Why?'

'At the moment, it is the only way I can think of to give in and save face both.'

Jack hugged her. She could feel he was laughing. 'Will you marry me?' he managed to ask solemnly.

Against his chest, Kathleen Murphy's red head slowly, deliberately nodded her yes.

Eight Day

Opening one eye, Sister Mary Helen squinted at her alarm clock. It was 5:30 a.m. She hadn't slept very well. She wasn't sure why. Maybe it was the Chinese food she had eaten with Kate and Jack last night. And there had been a little tension in the air while they were eating. Something was definitely wrong there. That bothered her a bit. But more than likely it was this murder business that was keeping her awake. 'The very air rests thick and heavily, where murder has been done.' That sounded like something Shakespeare might have said, although she knew he hadn't. For the life of her, however, she couldn't remember who had. Then there was this itch she had in the back of her mind, as if she were overlooking something. She couldn't put her finger on just what it was. Maybe that's why she wasn't sleeping.

Whatever the cause, she had tossed and fidgeted all night long. When she did sleep, she had awakened abruptly from outlandish dreams. The only one she could remember now was being chased by a group of Portuguese men with slanted eyes. They all brandished statues.

The dim flicker of daylight filled her small bedroom. Quietly, she rose and dressed. The desolate moan of the foghorn from the Gate warned her to put on her trench coat, the one with the fake fur lining.

Noiselessly, she pulled the heavy convent door closed behind her. The horns hadn't lied. A low, dense fog creeping up from the Bay had swallowed the hill, even dulling the gray-green of the floodlights surrounding the main building. Mary Helen shivered and put her hand up. She could see her hand in front of her face, but little else. Yet the wet mist against her face invigorated her.

This is probably a very foolish thing to do with all that's gone on around here, she speculated, but it feels so good. She breathed deeply. The cold air made her eyes water. Her nose felt wet.

Walking briskly away from the Sisters' Residence toward the side path leading to her favorite spot, she could almost hear Sister Therese hiss, 'Not only foolish, Sister dear, but downright dangerous.' This morning she didn't give a tinker's dam about danger. She needed to clear her head. 'Fear of danger is ten times more terrifying than danger itself!' As the shifting fog billowed around her, she hoped whoever said that was correct.

Low clumps of fog had completely swallowed the underbrush which bordered the side of the dirt path. Only an occasional spear of pampas grass pierced the denseness. It hung on the evergreen. The antiseptic smell of the tall, thin eucalyptus permeated the hillside.

Deliberately, Mary Helen trudged up the pathway, enjoying the steady, rhythmic crunch of her sturdy walking shoes digging into the dirt and gravel. Her mind picked up the beat. The kinks in her brain began to untwist. Crunch, crunch, crunch. Facts, motives, who? Facts, motives, who? Last evening she had told Kate, and that sweet Jack she lived with, about Tony's accosting her on the path. What had Kate said? 'Just a belligerent drunk.' Maybe so. Perhaps she had been wrong about him. An unlikely possibility — but one she had to admit to. Still, there was something cruel in the young man's eyes. Something about him . . . She could feel that itch begin again in the back of her mind. Maybe it had something to do with the possibility of two murderers.

Halfway up the hill, she stopped to catch her breath. Easy does it, old girl. You're not as young as you used to be, she reminded herself, leaning her hand against the stout trunk of an evergreen. Head bowed, she examined its rough bark.

Mary Helen bent forward and studied the bark more closely. A slash of dark, metallic green cut across the trunk as though something had scraped against it. What could it be? A car fender, perhaps. It was about the right height. But what in heaven's name would a car be doing on this narrow road?

With her thumbnail, Mary Helen flicked at the green. A small, incandescent chip stuck under her fingernail. It was metallic, all right! Dark green and metallic. A dark green car — where had she seen one recently? Mary Helen closed her eyes and jogged her memory. Then with frightening certainty she remembered. The professor's car, of course! She had heard the screeching tires on the service road and had seen it pull out behind a clump of trees and swerve on to the driveway. Professor Villanueva at the wheel, with another man beside him. Who was the other man? She wasn't sure. She had been so startled to see the professor that his passenger had simply been a blur! Could it have been his murderer?

Mary Helen removed the chip from under her fingernail and carefully wrapped it in a Kleenex. She'd give it to Kate just as soon as she saw her. This might be an important clue, and she certainly did not want to be accused of withholding evidence.

Almost imperceptibly, Mary Helen became aware of a slow, steady, grinding sound from the footpath. She listened. Who would be out walking this early in the morning? The sound was flat and quiet, as if someone were stealing toward her. It was not the carefree crunch that walking shoes made. Yet, it was rhythmic and definitely moving up the hill. She strained her eyes, but the dense fog blotted out all but a few feet in front of her.

She wanted to call out, but fear constricted her throat. Her dry mouth just wouldn't form the words. Yesterday's encounter with Tony flashed through her mind. What if Kate hadn't arrived just when she had? What might have happened? Would Tony have hurt her? Could this be Tony coming toward her? Or, if not Tony, maybe the murderer? The unidentified somebody they were all trying to find?

Legs trembling, Mary Helen clung to the gnarled tree trunk and stepped off the path into the underbrush. The prickly juniper scratched her trench coat and snagged her stockings. She crouched down. Her heart thumped in her ears. Breath came in quick, painful gasps.

The sound stopped right above her. Eyes closed, she hugged the side of the hill. All her muscles cramped. Without warning, the shale beneath her left foot gave way. She could feel herself slipping. Desperately, she grasped for the underbrush. Its shallow roots, wet with dripping fog, pulled away from the hillside.

Mary Helen lost her balance. Over and over she rolled. Small rocks and twigs scratched against her legs and hands. She could taste the fine-grained shower of loose rock cascading with her down the hillside.

A flat clearing stopped her fall. She lay there, dazed, as the last shower of dirt clattered in a cloud of dust around her.

'Who is that? Are you hurt?' She heard Anne's voice call down the hill from the pathway. For a moment, Mary Helen didn't know if she felt relieved or angry. Whichever, it was better than sickening fear. 'Are you all right?' Anne shouted.

'Dear Lord,' Mary Helen bargained before she opened her eyes, 'if I'm not dead, or at least maimed, I promise to start acting like a retired nun.' Even before she propped herself up on her elbows, she knew that neither the Lord nor she believed that.

Mary Helen opened her eyes and blinked. Miraculously, her glasses had not broken. Adjusting them, she watched Anne scurry down the side of the hill in her moccasins. Of course, that was the sound — Paiute moccasins! Mary Helen lay back on the ground, closed her eyes, and moaned.

'Mary Helen! Are you all right?' A worried Anne squatted down beside her. 'Spit,' she said, holding out the hankie she had taken from her car coat pocket. Adroitly, she dabbed at Mary Helen's cuts and bruises.

'What are you doing up so early?' Mary Helen asked.

'Couldn't sleep. And you?'

'Same.'

'Can you move everything?' Anne asked.

Slowly, painfully, Mary Helen tested her arms. They moved. Even though her stockings looked like spider webs, the legs underneath seemed to be intact.

Stiffly, she struggled to get up. 'Sit still for a while and take deep breaths.' Anne pretzled into her lotus position beside Mary Helen. 'Even if you have no broken bones, you've had quite a shock.'

'You can say that again.' Mary Helen ran her tongue across her teeth for a final check.

'How did you happen to tumble?' Anne helped her empty the grit from her shoes.

'You wouldn't believe it if I told you.' Mary Helen blinked back involuntary tears. 'Thank goodness for this flat clearing, or I could have kept on rolling.' She pressed her hands against the ground. They had begun to shake. Why, she might have been killed! Her life should have flashed before her. It didn't. In fact, she later admitted to Eileen, everything had happened so quickly that the only prayer she could think of was *Grace before Meals*.

Anne examined the clearing. 'Looks like someone has been digging here.' She pointed to the break where the smooth shale had been turned over.

'Tony,' Mary Helen answered flatly, still trying to steady her hands.

'That's some hole!' Mary Helen followed Anne's finger as she traced the perimeter of a large rectangle.

Mary Helen picked small pieces of rock from the heels of her hands. Here I am nearly dead, and she's talking about digging holes. Digging holes! With a sudden crash all her thoughts fell into place. She knew what it was that had been bothering her. Tony and his digging! She had seen him digging a huge hole to root ice plant. Ice plant only takes a shallow ditch! The freshly dug rectangle must be five or six feet long and a couple of feet wide. The size of a grave.

A sickening sensation rose in Mary Helen's throat. You would need a hole that large to bury someone. She put her hand over her mouth and fought down the urge to be sick. The color must have left her face, because Anne grabbed for her shoulders. And she had seen Tony digging several times! She retched.

'What is it?' Anne's hazel eyes were frightened behind her purple-rimmed glasses.

Mary Helen smiled weakly. 'Nothing,' she said, trying to sound calm. 'Help me up, will you, and let's get back to the college. I think I need a hot cup of coffee and a nice, long bath.'

'I have some herbal bath oil you can use,' Anne offered, gripping both her hands.

All I need now is to smell like oregano! Mary Helen let Anne pull her to her feet and silently lead her up the hillside toward the path.

'Dear Lord,' Mary Helen prayed silently, holding tight to Anne's hand, 'let it be my imagination — too many mystery novels, or something. It can't mean more dead bodies. Don't You know this is the eighth day of Therese's novena?' She felt a bit presumptuous asking God if He knew what day it was, but they did say there was no such thing as time in eternity. 'You are supposed to find the murderer, not more people who have been murdered!'

Panting, Mary Helen reached the path. Her whole body felt like a giant toothache. Small, dim slits of light floated through the dripping fog. Below them, the college was beginning to wake up.

★ ★ ★

Sister Mary Helen held her watch up to her ear. 'Still ticking.' She smiled sheepishly at Eileen. 'A watched pot never boils,' Eileen reminded her for the third time. For nearly an hour, the two had been huddled together sipping their early-morning coffee in the small nook off the kitchen. They were waiting for nine o'clock.

Right after the seven o'clock Sunday Mass, Mary Helen had run into Eileen. Although she had fully intended to keep her suspicions about the body-sized rectangle to herself, she was glad now she'd blurted them out. Misery loves company. One look at Eileen assured her that her friend was every bit as miserable as she was.

Eileen watched Mary Helen turn back her cuff and check her watch yet another time. 'For the love of all that's good and holy, why don't we just call?' she asked.

'Because I may be wrong. There is no sense disturbing someone so early on a Sunday morning if I'm wrong. And if I'm right, whoever it is will still be there, and none the worse for the wait.'

Eileen's soft-wrinkled face fell into a frown. 'There is a certain kind of logic that defies argument,' she said.

At the first stroke of nine, the two nuns shot from the nook. Clopping down the hallway, they left only the steady clinking of the loose hall tiles behind them.

By the time the college bell tolled the last stroke of nine, the two were in Eileen's office. Door closed, Mary Helen dialed Kate Murphy.

★ ★ ★

Inspector Gallagher stopped at the main gate just long enough for the two nuns to climb into the back seat. Slowly, the car labored up the steep grade.

'Here.' Mary Helen pointed to the narrow dirt path leading off from the paved driveway. Gallagher stopped the car.

'Isn't this the same path we met you and Tony on yesterday?' Kate turned toward the back seat.

Yes, Mary Helen nodded. Did she catch a hint of disbelief in Kate's voice? Did Kate think she was making all this up to prove a point?

'And what happened to your hands?' Kate noticed the scrapes. 'And is that a scratch on your face?'

'I had a tumble.' Mary Helen was not going to tell her what had really happened.

She'd certainly think it was all hysteria!

'Easy, Sisters.' Politely, Gallagher helped them from the car. Opening the trunk, he removed a shovel. 'You know, Sisters' — his watery-blue eyes studied them patiently — 'in these murder cases, sometimes our imaginations get the best of us. Run wild. We begin to see murders and murderers everywhere.'

So he didn't believe her, either. Maybe your imagination is unreliable, but mine is tried and true, thank you, Mary Helen thought. Deliberately, she pointed to the rough trunk of the evergreen.

'This morning I also noticed that scrape. Metallic paint, I think. A car, probably. Although I have no idea why a car would be on this footpath.' Adjusting her bifocals, she stared at Gallagher. So much for overworked imagination!

Simultaneously, Kate and Gallagher bent forward to examine the green slash. 'I removed a chip' — she handed the Kleenex to Kate — 'and the rectangle I spoke to you about is right down there.'

'You two go sit on the bench,' Kate ordered as she and Gallagher clambered down the embankment. 'We'll let you know the minute we find anything.'

Obediently, the two nuns sat freezing on the cold stone bench. A gray blanket of fog still wrapped the city.

'This is a beautiful view, when you can see it.' Mary Helen tried to make small talk. Funny how people always tried to make small talk when faced with overwhelming situations. She was no exception.

'I think I see the top of City Hall.' Eileen pointed to her left.

'I hope none of the nuns walk out this way.'

'No one in her right mind would walk out here in this cold. If they are doing anything, they are probably having a second cup of good, hot coffee.' Eileen shivered.

'Where's Anne?'

'She had an appointment with Marina. Apparently it was something quite important. She left right after Mass.'

'Marina! Is Anne alone?'

'Of course she's alone. Why do you ask?'

'I don't want to be an alarmist, but we really don't have any idea who the murderer is.' Or even if there is more than one. She kept that thought to herself. 'It could be Marina as well as anyone else,' she said.

Eileen frowned. 'I don't care what you say about Cain and Abel. I just cannot believe Marina would kill her own sister!'

'Maybe not, but until we know for sure, I think it is foolish and downright dangerous for Anne to be out there alone!'

Eileen stared at her friend in amazement. 'Well, if this isn't a typical case of the pot calling the kettle black, old dear,' she said, 'then I've never seen one!'

Impatiently, Mary Helen walked to the edge of the clearing and looked down at the two inspectors. Gallagher had removed his jacket and was heaving great shovelfuls of dirt from one corner. Kate stood next to him, holding his jacket and peering into the freshly dug hole.

Abruptly, Inspector Gallagher stopped. On hands and knees, Kate inspected his hole. She mumbled something Mary Helen could not hear. Gallagher shook his head, then helped her to her feet.

'Looks like you were right,' Kate cupped her hands and hollered up.

It was the first time in a long while that Mary Helen could remember not wanting to be right.

★ ★ ★

Within minutes, the entire hillside had been cordoned off. 'This looks like something right out of the *Streets of San Francisco*.' Mary Helen pointed to the black-and-white patrol cars lining the driveway. Their circling red-and-blue lights cut through the fog.

Police radios squawked. Floodlights threw broad beams across the misty clearing. A police ambulance whooped up the hill, followed closely by the coroner and several men carrying metal cases. Crime Lab, Mary Helen thought. Finally, the inevitable van marked 'Channel 4 — On the Scene' turned in from Turk Street and pulled behind the last patrol car. A jeans-clad, bearded fellow jumped from one door. Hoisting a heavy television camera to his shoulder, he followed a trim, smartly dressed woman. Mary Helen recognized her as one of the reporters from the five o'clock news. Poor Cecilia!

'You two might as well go to the convent and keep warm. There's nothing else you can do up here,' Kate said. She walked several feet down the path with the two nuns.

'Have you any idea who's buried there?' Mary Helen asked.

Kate shook her head. 'Whoever it is hasn't been dead too long,' she said. 'We'll get the body out and downtown to be identified. Denny and I are going to pick up Tony. There are some questions we want to ask him. I'll keep you posted.'

Kate turned to walk away. Unexpectedly, she swung around. 'By the way, is there anything else you'd like to mention before I go?' She leveled her eyes at Mary Helen.

'Well, there is something.' Mary Helen swallowed hard, hesitant even to admit the possibility to herself. 'I've seen Tony digging in several other spots.'

Kate's face blanched.

★ ★ ★

Right after the evening news, Mary Helen ran into Sister Anne. Head down, the young nun tried to slide past.

'Are you all right?' Mary Helen asked. One glimpse at Anne's red-rimmed eyes and death-white face told her that it was a silly question.

'Fine. Just tired.' Anne moved rapidly toward the front staircase.

'Are you sure? Did something happen with Marina?'

'Nothing happened,' Anne snapped. 'I'm fine. Just tired,' she said, without turning around.

While Mary Helen was debating whether or not to follow Anne up to her bedroom, the phone rang.

It was Kate Murphy. 'Are you watching TV?' she asked.

'Just finished.' Mary Helen's knees were still weak from the sight of hefty patrolmen struggling up the embankment with a bloated bag on a stretcher — not once, but four times! She still couldn't believe it. The whole thing was like a horrible nightmare.

'Thanks be to God,' Eileen had muttered when the fourth stretcher appeared. Mary Helen had looked at her friend aghast. 'Death always comes in threes,' Eileen explained. 'Six means it is all over.'

'Sorry I didn't get back to you sooner,' Kate continued. 'I guess you saw that they uncovered four bodies. Things moved fast after you left.'

'Have you any idea who they are? Are they the four missing Portuguese boys?'

'All we know so far is that they are male and Caucasian. Coroner is still working on positive I.D.s. Also, we sent that paint to the lab. Nothing, so far. Denny and I are just back from picking up Tony. We're just about to start the interrogation. I'll call you tomorrow. And, Sister' — Kate's voice had a tired ring — 'thanks. And for heaven's sake, tonight sleep well.'

As she opened the door of the phone booth, Mary Helen could hear Sister Therese's staccato steps coming toward her.

'Imagine! Now it is 'Homicidal Maniac Haunts Holy Hill'!' Therese rounded the corner waving the front page of the

Chronicle. Her high-pitched voice filled the corridor. 'Disgraceful! Disgusting! Dastardly!'

'But, you mark my words.' She shook her thin, arthritic forefinger at Sister Mary Helen. 'Tomorrow is the last day of my novena, and we'll have one haunting homicidal maniac in harness!'

Ninth Day

It was the first time in anyone's memory that classes at the college had been cancelled. Rescheduled, yes. But cancelled — never! Sister Cecilia had made the announcement with a quivering voice.

A heavy, silent gloom hung over the deserted campus. The largest gray stone building loomed on the hilltop like an abandoned castle left to ruin. The gargoyles set in the majestic stonework frowned into space. Even the bright yellow primroses bordering the formal gardens drooped.

Sister Therese was desolate. Not a single soul, not even Mary Helen, ventured to mention her novena. 'A despicable day in the history of this college,' Therese had proclaimed at breakfast. No one had disagreed.

Unfortunately, someone had forgotten to inform the sun. It rose gloriously cheerful 'with all his beams full-dazzling.' Mary Helen stepped out of the Sisters' Residence. She watched the warm, golden halo cover the hill and make it sparkle. Where in the world was the fog when you needed it?

She stretched. In spite of everything, she

had slept soundly. What was it Cervantes had written? 'So long as I am asleep, I have neither fear nor hope, trouble nor glory.' Yet, she woke still tired. Slowly, she rambled up the driveway. Every part of her hurt. You can't expect to roll down a hill at your age, old girl, and never feel a twinge, she had reminded herself this morning when she pulled her two stiff knees out of bed.

The dirt path was still cordoned off. Several official-looking cars parked along the driveway reminded her that the Crime Lab was still at work. Probably sifting through tons of dirt looking for she wasn't sure what. Clues, no doubt, to link someone with these heinous murders. What a job, she thought, peering down the embankment.

It was difficult — no, impossible — to see what the men were doing from the driveway. Mary Helen pulled up the thick rope and was just about to duck under when she heard Eileen call her name.

'For the love of all that's good and holy, you aren't going in there, are you?' Eileen's gray eyes registered horror.

Mary Helen released the rope. 'Don't be ridiculous!'

'We are both wanted in the parlor. It's Kate Murphy,' Eileen announced, watching the rope bounce.

'I wonder what she wants.'

'I have no idea. But they have a saying in the old country which I think fits this situation perfectly. 'Just keep a cool head and dry pants, and you'll be fine.''

Mary Helen stared at her friend. In all the years she'd known Eileen, she had never heard her quote that saying before. But these were quite unusual times!

The two hurried down the driveway. Mary Helen was puffing by the time she and Eileen sank into the over-stuffed parlor couch.

'Good morning, Sisters.' Every freckle stood out on Kate Murphy's white face. Her eyes, red-rimmed from lack of sleep, shifted uneasily. 'I have some good news and some bad news.'

'Let's hear the good news first.' Eileen leaned over and patted Kate's hand. You could always count on Eileen to be optimistic. Mary Helen wished they would rid themselves of the bad news first.

'Well, we questioned Tony for hours. Gallagher and I. First, I played the good guy, he was the tough cop. Then we switched. Finally, Tony broke. I think he was actually glad to get it off his chest. It's some story.'

The two nuns inched up to the edge of the couch waiting for Kate to continue.

'Seems you were right all along, Sister Mary Helen. The professor, this Sebastiao business, and Joanna were all tied in. Apparently, Professor Villanueva was a real bast . . . ' She caught herself. 'A character. Made trips to the old country. Put himself up as a savior.

'That Dom Sebastiao-reincarnated business you were telling me about. It's a screwy cult that never seems to quite die out in Portugal. It rises every so often among the young men who can't help hoping that Sebastiao will return and lead the country to glory, plus take a few of them along on his coat tails. Guess it happens every place.

'Anyway, this guy convinced them that he was their ticket to fame and riches. They could really make something of themselves. First thing he did was bring them to the U.S. without benefit of the Immigration Department.'

'And all for a price, you can be sure.' Eileen shook her head disapprovingly.

'Quite a price, we found out from Luis, your janitor. What he didn't tell us was that none of them could afford the whole thing, so they had to borrow from the professor, at a huge interest. They would be working to pay him back for years and years.'

Eileen could hardly believe it. 'Sounds like

a combination of loan shark and indentured servant,' she said.

'And the men he duped were only a beginning. If he could bring three or four more over every year and have them repay him, with all the money tax free, in no time at all the man would have a very lucrative business going.

'But these guys were merely poor, not stupid. They weren't here very long before they realized they were getting nowhere fast. They began to demand a little something back and *adeus*!' Kate pulled her forefinger across her throat.

'Himself?' Mary Helen was aghast to think of the meticulously groomed professor with the practiced smile slitting someone's throat.

Kate shook her head. 'Dirty his fingernails? Never! He had Tony take care of it. Stalk, kill, and bury. All for one fee.'

'Why Tony?'

'Seems Tony killed a man in a drunken brawl in Santa Clara. At least, the professor told him he had. Tony couldn't remember. We'll have to check it out. Villanueva claimed he covered up for him, so the professor had Tony right where he wanted him. The guy was desperate. I don't think his heart was ever really in it.'

'And there is no accuser so terrible as the

conscience that dwells in the heart of every man.' Sister Mary Helen remembered some Roman or other had said that in the first century, but she couldn't, for the life of her, remember which one.

Eileen shuddered. 'Why would anyone in his right mind do such a thing?'

'Simple,' Kate said. 'Greed.'

Lucre, Mary Helen thought, relieved the motive wasn't loathing. All along, Leonel had weighed a little heavily on the loathing. She really should not have worried, however. She had seen it all in the eyes: the professor's, Leonel's, and finally, Tony's. Those fifty years in the classroom had, indeed, stood her in good stead. One good look, and she could spot innocence or malevolence instantly. She was glad she hadn't lost her touch!

'Have you identified the bodies yet?' Mary Helen asked.

'Not officially. But Tony told us who they were. By the way, I'd appreciate it if tomorrow you could go with me to see Senhora Rubiero.'

'Her two nephews?' Mary Helen sucked in her breath.

'Plus the two Manuels we were looking for.'

'How does Joanna fit in?' Eileen asked.

'Joanna and her sister were a different story. They did have legal papers. For some reason, the professor didn't want to mess with them.'

'Leonel did mention that in the village, they were richer and better educated than most,' Mary Helen said.

'Maybe the professor was afraid the family would make trouble.'

'He couldn't exploit them nor blow his cover by not sponsoring them.' Mary Helen was getting into the spirit of the thing.

'Anyway. It was Joanna's thesis on Portuguese immigrants that got her into trouble. When she went looking for primary sources and how well her subject adjusted to life in the United States, she found out too much for her own good.'

'We'll never know exactly what made her suspicious,' Mary Helen said. 'All the copies have disappeared.

'Even my library copy,' Eileen added.

'I suppose he thought that if Joanna could stumble on to his scheme, someone else reading the thesis might do the same.'

Kate nodded.

'Anyway, after the thesis was finished, she decided to do something about the abuses. When she went back to find these fellows for the second time, they had disappeared.'

'And of course, she got suspicious — went to check it out with the relatives.'

'The little dots on her list!' Eileen beamed.

'Right. What Kevin Doherty told you was correct. When Joanna went to see Senhora Rubiero, she finally realized something was not jibing. She probably guessed what it was. Unfortunately, she told her suspicions to Tony.' Kate faced Sister Mary Helen. 'As a matter of fact, the day you saw him kiss her, she had just come upon him digging a grave.'

'For whom?' Mary Helen could feel a tingle race up her spine.

'For Leonel,' she said. 'Tony tried to persuade her to join him. You were right, Sister. She hated Tony. So he had no choice but to kill her. She knew that.'

'And is that why the poor girl disappeared?' Eileen asked.

'Yes. She was scared to death. And with good reason. Knew he'd look for her at home. So she must have gone into hiding.

'Then she made her fatal mistake.'

'What was that?'

'Instead of calling us, she came back to the college. We don't know why. Tony came upon her, bashed her skull with his shovel. Didn't have time for his usual throat-slitting. Waited all day to stuff her body in the chapel.'

Eileen gasped. 'Then that's who I must have seen on the hillside,' she said. 'Do you remember?' She turned toward her friend. 'It was the foggy morning we were going to see Leonel in jail. If we had only . . . '

'There's lots of 'ifs,' Sister,' Kate said.

Mary Helen eased herself back into a more comfortable position. She felt drained. 'Why didn't he just bury her with the rest?' she asked.

'This part is hard to swallow, but he loved her and wanted her to be buried in the church. Funeral Mass, Christian burial, the whole schmeer.'

'I guess no one is all bad.' Eileen blinked.

'And the chip of paint?'

'The lab is still checking it out. Probably from the professor's car. These guys had their own hearse service.'

'But then, why the professor? Why kill the hand that feeds you?' Mary Helen twisted the old adage a bit, but the point was clear.

'That's the bad news. Tony claims, vehemently, that he did not kill the professor.'

'Maybe it was an accident, then?'

'No. Coroner says that's impossible.'

A sharp, unsettling pain shot through the bottom of Sister Mary Helen's stomach, like the end of an elevator ride. So her worst fears were true. There were two murderers! 'Who do you think it is, then?'

Before Kate could answer, a soft, persistent

knocking began on the parlor door. Cautiously, Mary Helen opened it.

Anne, eyes bleary, black hair uncombed, stood with her slender arm around Marina. The young woman, her delicate face drawn, fumbled with a wadded Kleenex. Her eyes were swollen from crying. Anne eased her into the room. 'Marina has something to tell you,' she said.

'I killed him,' Marina blurted out before anyone had time even to ask *what*?

'Killed whom?' Kate asked softly.

'Professor Villanueva.'

Methodically, Kate read Marina her rights.

'But I want to tell you about it,' Marina burst in. Her face looked set in stone. 'I did it. I killed him. That animal wanted to destroy my Leonel.'

'Did you know this?' Kate turned toward Sister Anne.

'Not till last night. Marina had to tell someone.'

'Why didn't you call me immediately?'

'It was a confidence. Believe me, I wrestled with it all night. This morning I persuaded Marina to tell you.' Anne glanced at the young woman. 'May I?'

Marina nodded her head. 'Go ahead,' Kate said.

'Seems our Professor Villanueva had helped

Leonel emigrate. Promised him Marina,' she said. 'When Leonel came to talk to the professor about the papers that would enable him to marry legally in this country, he hedged. Leonel became suspicious. Not only of him and his dealings, but of what had happened to his friends from home. Joanna had mentioned something to him. Anyway, the night of the earthquake, he and Marina had decided to confront Villanueva. Lionel became violently angry, lunged for the man's throat. The professor pulled a knife. He meant to use it. Marina was behind, and bashed him with the first thing handy. The statue. Leonel grabbed it from her to strike again, but just then the earthquake hit.'

Standing there, mutely, next to Anne, Marina looked so fragile, so helpless. Yet Mary Helen remembered her strong hands and that glint of steel in her eyes. She had needed that strength to kill, not like Cain and Abel, but more like David slaying the giant Goliath. The scene in the professor's office must have been horrible!

And the presence she had sensed in the darkened hallway. Why, that had been Leonel, of course.

'Why didn't they say something sooner?' Kate asked.

'Frightened of the police, of the system, of

deportation.' Anne looked at Marina tenderly. 'They decided the earthquake was an act of God. They left the statue on the ground, but were so distraught they totally forgot the prints.'

'And the knife? What happened to the knife?'

'Leonel just slipped it back in a kitchen drawer with all the other knives.'

'I'm sure they would have come to the police eventually,' Anne said. 'In fact, after the professor's death, they went through his office trying to find a copy of Joanna's thesis, but all the copies had been destroyed.'

Mary Helen fidgeted uncomfortably. 'What will happen now?' she asked, eager to get off the subject of the professor's office. No sense in bringing that up.

'I don't know. It will be up to the D.A. and the Immigration Service.' Kate stood up. 'I'll have to take her in,' she said gently.

For a moment, Marina cringed in the corner like a frightened child, but only for a moment. Then, squaring her shoulders, she wiped her eyes and stepped forward. Mary Helen recognized a survivor. Good for her!

Epilogue

Sister Eileen pulled open the heavy bronze doors of the college chapel and hooked them back.

'Glory be to God, it is almost full!' She tugged at Sister Mary Helen's new blue jacket. 'And we still have fifteen minutes to go. Here, look.'

Sure enough, the nave of the large gothic chapel was almost completely filled. An interesting assortment, Mary Helen noted. Portuguese and policemen, peppered with nuns. They sat in friendly clusters chatting softly. Sister Cecilia walked down the aisle like a political candidate, smiling, nodding, shaking hands. Everything was running smoothly once more.

Mary Helen waved back to Mrs Rubiero, who had spotted her immediately. The poor woman had taken the news of the deaths of her two nephews quite bravely. The old nun was glad to see that Luis had escorted her to this wedding. And wasn't that Kevin Doherty's blonde head bobbing up in the crowd? Nice boy, she thought. Glad he came.

'Don't you just love a November wedding?'

Sister Therese gushed. 'Although I sincerely hope Sister Eileen doesn't throw rice all over the chapel floor. It is dangerous, you know.' Eileen had insisted that a wedding without the good luck that rice brings would be far more dangerous than somebody taking a tumble.

'Look at the lovely mums.' Therese pointed to the large baskets of yellow and white spider chrysanthemums banking the main altar. Clicking down the middle aisle, she squeezed into a seat at the end of one of the front pews.

Sister Mary Helen looked. For once, she had to agree with Therese. The altar did look lovely. Anne and a group of students were to the left of it, setting up music and tuning their guitars. Why, Anne even was wearing a skirt and had traded her Paiutes for sandals!

Mary Helen loved weddings, anybody's wedding. But today's were especially special. Today she felt a little like the mother of the bride. Or in this case, brides.

With a flurry of activity, the bridal party arrived in the hallway outside the chapel doors. Marina, her hair framing her delicate face, floated in on a cloud of chiffon. Leonel, tall, muscular, clung to her hand. 'Hi, Sisters.' He flashed his wide smile.

'You look lovely,' Eileen said, squeezing Marina. 'And you, too.' Turning, she squeezed

Kate Murphy. 'And the weather is cooperating! 'Blessed the bride that the sun shines on!''

Kate nodded, laughing. A soft, blue gown swirled around her slim figure and accented the Wedgwood blue of her eyes. She leaned her head against Jack's shoulder. He kissed the top of it, then grinned. A little, Mary Helen thought, like the cat who had just swallowed the canary.

'Get a load of my mother,' Jack whispered. 'Front pew.' Mary Helen stretched to see. The short, round, silver-haired woman hugging the end of the pew was dabbing her eyes.

'She started crying the minute I picked her up this morning,' he said. 'If we don't start this wedding on time, I'm afraid she'll drown.'

'Sisters, I'd like you to meet my wife,' Gallagher interrupted, nodding toward the slim, attractive gray-haired woman straightening his tie.

Mrs Gallagher turned and smiled. 'I've heard a lot about you: Denny told me what a help you were in solving the Holy Hill murder case.' She brushed several tiny specks of ash from the front of her husband's jacket. 'He thinks you should have been mentioned in the commendation he and Kate received.'

Planting a light kiss on Gallagher's cheek, Mrs G. hurried down the main aisle to a place near the front.

Eileen checked the big clock in the hall. 'Five minutes to go,' she warned.

'Have you heard anything about Leonel's and Marina's cases yet?' Mary Helen covered her mouth and whispered to Kate.

'Self-defense. It's up to Immigration now. I think it will all work out. The press has really done a job on Professor Villanueva and his activities. And the whole city is crazy about our friends here. They've become heroes.'

'So what guy from Immigration is going to have the guts to throw a hero and his heroine out of the country?' Jack added.

Kate turned toward him. 'Even if they are deported, they might as well go back as husband and wife.'

'Poor guy couldn't wait much longer.' Jack gave Kate a knowing smile.

'Gentlemen, take your places,' Eileen ordered.

The two grooms rushed down the hallway toward the side door of the sacristy.

'See you in church,' Jack called over his shoulder.

Clutching her sack of rice, Eileen hurried up a side aisle toward her place.

The folk group strummed the opening

chords of the entrance hymn. Gallagher, a bride on either arm, straightened his shoulders, preparing to follow. Sister Mary Helen took her first solemn step down the long center aisle of the college chapel.

This is ridiculous, she thought, clinging to her small bouquet. Whoever heard of a seventy-five-year-old flower girl!

We do hope that you have enjoyed reading this large print book.

Did you know that all of our titles are available for purchase?

We publish a wide range of high quality large print books including:
Romances, Mysteries, Classics
General Fiction
Non Fiction and Westerns

Special interest titles available in large print are:
The Little Oxford Dictionary
Music Book
Song Book
Hymn Book
Service Book

Also available from us courtesy of Oxford University Press:
Young Readers' Dictionary
(large print edition)
Young Readers' Thesaurus
(large print edition)

For further information or a free brochure, please contact us at:
Ulverscroft Large Print Books Ltd.,
The Green, Bradgate Road, Anstey,
Leicester, LE7 7FU, England.
Tel: (00 44) 0116 236 4325
Fax: (00 44) 0116 234 0205

Other titles published by
The House of Ulverscroft:

THE LONG DEAD

John Dean

When sixteen skeletons are unearthed near an old prisoner-of-war camp outside the northern city of Hafton, it seems like a straightforward case for Detective Chief Inspector John Blizzard. With all indicators pointing to natural deaths from influenza during the Second World War, there seems little to concern modern-day detectives. But Blizzard's instincts tell him something is wrong. As he investigates the case alongside his colleague, Sergeant David Colley, they find themselves revealing dark secrets concealed for more than fifty years. And for John Blizzard it'll mean confronting demons from his own past.

THE WIDOW'S TALE

Margaret Frazer

Spring 1449. When Cristiana Helyngton's husband dies, her greedy relatives are determined to have control of her lands and her daughters. Imprisoned, she must save herself before she can save her children. For Dame Frevisse at St Frideswide's nunnery, Cristiana is merely a puzzle, but then questions rise and troubles turn deadly. In England, civil war looms when the corrupt king's men face opposition. Cristiana must use a secret entrusted to her by her husband — a secret with power to destroy even those most dear to her. Drawn ever deeper into trouble, Frevisse must decide where her loyalties lie.

THE TOOTH OF TIME

Sue Henry

Enjoying the prospect of adventure, sixty-something-year-old Maxie McNabb zigzags across the country in her Winnebago. With her canine companion, Stretch, they head for New Mexico, where Maxie plans to learn how to weave. But everything changes when a local woman attempts suicide. A casualty of her husband's midlife crisis, she has been replaced by a newer, sexier model. And to top it off, a conman is targeting her. Now, Maxie is determined to help, and with her nose for trouble, she'll leave no stone unturned until she brings two dogs to justice — neither of which is Stretch!

SECONDHAND SMOKE

Karen E. Olson

Reporter Annie Seymour investigates a suspicious fire in a neighborhood-favorite Italian restaurant. A body is found in the rubble, the restaurant owner is missing and the FBI is involved. Annie begins to realise that she's an outsider in her own neighborhood, searching for a way in. She is forced to question some of the very people who watched her grow up, from opinionated Italian mothers to a retired Mafia godfather with active mob connections. And at every turn, Annie keeps bumping into heartthrob P.I. Vinny DeLucia — a mixed-up romance that only makes her task even more difficult.

LET ME DIE YESTERDAY

Theresa Murphy

When hired to trace a village girl who went missing in the 1960s, private investigator Gerry McCabe anticipates an early end to his assignment with the discovery of female remains. Instead, it plunges McCabe into the dark and hostile labyrinths of rural life. Intent on mending his broken marriage, he is distracted by the vivacious Beth Merrill — the missing girl's sister — and the alluring widow Sharee Bucholtz. Unwittingly causing a local tragedy, a distraught McCabe struggles to continue his investigation and resolve his own relationship difficulties. But can he succeed on either case?

THE EDGE

Clare Curzon

A banging barn door in the middle of the night disturbs farm manager Ned Barton, who discovers the body of a woman displayed on straw bales, like a sacrificial trophy. Superintendent Mike Yeadings of the Thames Valley police is faced with multiple murder as three more bodies are discovered in the manor house: an entire family massacred, except for a missing boy. Village gossip suggests an occult element. Then an eccentric grandmother presents herself as the boy's legal guardian. As Yeadings unearths deeper layers of mystery he must lead his team through the mental labyrinth to find the perpetrator.

Sister Carol Anne O'Marie has been a Sister of St Joseph of Carondelet for over forty years. She ministers to homeless women at a drop-in centre in downtown Oakland, California, which she co-founded in 1990.